Little Lies and Serious Indiscretions

....

short stories

Little Lies and Serious Indiscretions

short stories

Beverly Olevin

Marley Publishing

Los Angeles

MARLEY PUBLISHING

Los Angeles, CA

info@marleyarts.com

Book design by Marc Olevin
Text set in Minion Pro

Beverly Olevin
Visit my website at www.beverlyolevin.com

Printed in the United States of America

First Printing: September 2012

For Marc, my rock and soul
who makes me laugh every day.

Ask me no questions
I'll tell you no lies.

—Oliver Goldsmith
She Stoops to Conquer

....

No mask like open truth to cover lies,
as to go naked is the best disguise.

—William Congreve
The Double Dealer

Contents

Little Lies and Serious Indiscretions

....

short stories

Following Bennie

"What have you got there?" Her tone had a decidedly acerbic quality, as if she were talking to an annoying, slow-witted child. "What are you doing with that red umbrella!"

Stanley, her husband of twenty-eight years, pulled back, a defensive move, but he left open the option to attack if a second advance should occur. She noted the slight tension, the constricting in the loose skin around his temples. His deferring nature had been eroding of late and she wasn't interested in provoking an argument today.

"The Today Show said it was going to rain," Stanley proclaimed, bringing all the forces of network meteorology to his aid. "A front is coming in this afternoon."

"It is a perfectly glorious day," Mary Ann retorted. She was willing to bend but she could not indulge him altogether. "Why don't you look outside instead of looking at the television?"

To prove her point she marched through the entryway and swung the front door open. "See, lovely. Feel that warm sun. Put the umbrella away," she instructed him.

Stanley glanced through the door at the sparkling day. She did have reality on her side. The sky was cloudless. In the living room Willard Scott was extolling the beauty of a 104-year- old prune-faced woman who was cowering in front of a blazing birthday cake. Stanley's resolve faded. She was right. Obediently, he returned the umbrella to its assigned hook in the cloak closet.

Partly to reward him for his good behavior and partly to keep the advantage, Mary Ann took a different tact. "Even if it were to rain, dear, I'm sure you couldn't be thinking of taking a red umbrella to a funeral."

Again she was right. Countless funeral scenes he had watched in films played across the screen of his imagination — the casket carried through the gray drizzling rain, the mourners holding up their wide black umbrellas, the camera slowly panning away from the gathering crowd, the view from above. So pleasing, so harmonious.

"I don't think these earrings work."

He looked over at his wife, who was studying her reflection in the brass-framed mirror in the foyer. He had to admit she was still an attractive woman even in her funeral attire, a tailored black suit with a mid-calf length skirt covering her long slender legs. The years and her five mile morning walks had been good to her, and to him too. For the first twenty-five years of his marriage he watched his wife march out the door at 6:30 a.m., her face set against the morning chill, without the layers of creams, powders and eye make-up that would hide her soft Iowa-born features for the rest of the day. Her stride already brisk before she hit the sidewalk. For an hour and a half he could sit at the breakfast table, reading the paper from cover to cover, drinking coffee, his mind wandering without purpose or direction. This was precious time before his wife's return, before the chair opposite him would house a daily mantra of accusations that his life lacked drive or ambition. Three years ago this litany had coalesced into a single demand: he was to join her on those early morning forced marches. The exercise would serve to thin his ever increasing waist and fill him with more energy for the day ahead. He didn't have the energy to fight her, so now as a result, unlike most men in their mid-fifties, his belt still fit comfortably across a flat stomach. No, he wasn't complaining: he was in good shape. His friends told him this often with a trace of jealousy in their voices.

It was, by all measures, true. In a quiet sort of way, his life was a thing to be envied. But in this moment, watching his wife carefully tighten the barrette that held her hair back from her face, he didn't want to think of his life as a thing, and he didn't feel desirous of anyone's envy.

Mary Ann Watersmith released the tiny black pearl earrings she had purchased last Christmas as a gift from her husband. "I'm going to change earrings," she told Stanley as if it were a matter that closely concerned him. "The diamond studs will work better," she concluded, disappointed to abandon the pearls. They had been so expensive and she had been waiting for an occasion to wear them. Reluctantly she turned and climbed the stairs to their bedroom. He watched her go, gracefully ascending, her skirt swirling around her small hips. Yes, he liked her body, but perhaps, he thought, she liked it quite a bit more than he did. Some matronly filling out would have been fine with him — a slight rounding in the stomach, a softness in the thighs.

An impulse came to Stanley as she disappeared from his view on the landing above. He returned to the closet, slipped the red umbrella under his arm and shouted up to his wife, "I'll wait for you in the car, dear."

Once in the garage he opened the trunk and hid the red umbrella under the plaid blanket they kept for the possibility of a spontaneous picnic. He had suggested putting the blanket there the day after they bought the Volvo three years ago. It had never left the trunk. He saw Mary Ann hurrying towards the car just as he opened the driver's side door.

"You do have the address, don't you?" she asked, her tone implying that it would be just like him to forget it. "I don't want to be late. These things always start on time."

Stanley pulled his seat belt across his chest and turned on the engine, letting it idle for a minute or so. He could see that Mary Ann was annoyed having to sit still and waste time on something she thought was unnecessary. Even the salesman had agreed with here—the Volvo didn't require time to warm-up. But Stanley liked sitting in the car for a moment before pushing his foot against the gas pedal. He liked the sound of the motor humming peacefully before it knew its purpose or direction.

"I have the address," he said, placing the card announcing the funeral on the dashboard.   The leaves on the maple trees were beginning to turn. If they weren't going to a funeral, Stanley thought, it might have been a fine day for a picnic.

"Do you remember what your Uncle Bennie was like when you were a child?"

She uncrossed her legs and folded her hands, with their freshly polished nails, in her lap.   Several minutes passed so Stanley assumed Mary Ann hadn't been listening to him.

"Yes, I do," she said finally. Her voice took on a soft quality that Stanley hadn't heard for years. "I will always remember Bennie. He brought me a mask when he came back from Africa. I was ten years old. It was made of wood and tree bark. There was red paint around the eye holes, like blood. He held it up in front of his face and danced around my bedroom, chanting like a wild native. At first I was frightened, but he took my hand and showed me how to move my feet as he did. Then he gave me the mask to put in front of my face. Looking up at him through those holes, he was the most wonderful and exciting person I ever knew."

Stanley tried to imagine his wife, a child of ten, playing with her eccentric uncle, but the picture eluded him. "He traveled a lot even then?" Stanley asked, wishing he could see Bennie right now, not as he was last spring when they visited him in the rest home, but as a young man dancing with an authentic African mask over his face.

"The man was crazy." Mary Ann pulled down the sun visor and checked her make-up in the mirror. "No one ever knew where he was or what he was doing. I don't think he ever had a real job in his life."

"But when you were a child did you think he was crazy?" Stanley suddenly needed to know not just who Bennie was forty years ago, but what the young Mary Ann was like in his company.

"What does a child know? He would just pop in every few years, stay with us for a while, and then disappear again. He was my mother's brother, but she was never happy to see him. She said he was disruptive to our lives. He filled our heads with wild stories and we would be intoxicated with them for months after he left."

A young Mary Ann intoxicated with fantastic tales of a man's wanderings — the image excited Stanley. He could see her sitting on Uncle Bennie's knee begging him to tell her more. But he didn't want to be a voyeur in his wife's childhood bedroom, an invisible presence, a shadow from her future traveling back in time. Stanley wanted to be Bennie. He wanted to have been the one who sent those postcards from exotic places all over the world that Mary Ann still kept in a box on the top shelf of their closet.

The day before the funeral, Stanley had waited excitedly for Mary Ann's three o'clock appointment to get her hair done before the service. With her out of the house, he figured he would have a good few hours to look inside that box, at the world that belonged to Bennie. A cascade of dust came down with the box as he lowered it from its long resting place at the back of the top shelf. Sitting on their bed he carefully put all the postcards in chronological order, worried that this task alone would eat up too much time, that any moment he would hear the garage door open and Mary Ann would advance into the bedroom, her blond hair stiffly coiffed and pulled tightly back off her face, looking to him exactly the same as before she had left for the beauty salon. But his fears were unfounded, the house remained silent.

He began turning over the postcards, discovering a tiny adventure on each one. In simple sentences written to a young girl, Bennie told of trekking through the Pyrenees, rock climbing on the Tors of Southern Ireland, drinking with his mates at Oktoberfest in Heidelberg. After a dozen or so cards, Stanley began to move inside the photo on the postcard until he was part of a wonderful adventure. He began envisioning himself traveling alongside Bennie, joking with him and his mates about the damn mosquitoes the size of bats swarming around them as they sailed down the Amazon. It didn't take much to get Stanley's imagination running wild. A picture postcard of a row of houses all painted white lying on the blue of the Aegean was enough to get him spinning a marvelous tale of how he and Bennie were drinking Ouzo and sleeping in a cave on Crete after swimming naked in the sea at midnight. Never mind that the message on the back of the card read, Sweet Mary Ann, I thought of you today when I was diving in this cove. You would have loved the parrotfish I saw. Someday I'll bring you here and we will see these bird fish together. Love, Uncle Bennie.

A picture of the Tower of London had been taken at dusk. Stanley surmised the camera had been suspended from a hovering helicopter, perhaps sent by Scotland Yard to search the whereabouts of the two men suspected of hiding in the Tower. Bennie and Stanley had made their way up the heavy stone stairs to the famous rooms where Anne Boleyn contemplated the axe that was about to fall across her neck. A thin mist fell from the ceiling as they entered the room and formed itself in the doomed girl's image, her ghost reaching out to them, imploring them to rescue her in first-rate fairy tale fashion. Silly, Stanley thought, as he dropped the image and turned to the next postcard. His life, when compared to Bennie's, was a collection of details and small cautious moments.

Traffic was exceptionally light even for a Sunday, so the Watersmiths arrived twenty minutes before the service was scheduled to begin making them the first mourners at the scene. The sign that usually announced the title of the sermon now simply read:

Funeral — Two p.m. — Benjamin Jay Gladstone.

Together they walked inside to find Saint Catherine's completely empty. Stanley thought the grand cathedral seemed cavernous without anyone in the pews. Even the priest was nowhere to be found. They were alone except for Uncle Bennie. The closed casket had already been placed in front of the altar.

Since Stanley had been imagining his adventures with Bennie much of the drive, he was quite happy to have this time alone with the leading character of his fantasy. But Mary Ann was not pleased with this moment of solitude. "My God," she exclaimed, quite forgetting that she was taking the Lord's name in vain in a church. "What if no one comes?" The idea overwhelmed her and she dropped to a seat at the back of the cathedral.

"Of course someone will come," he assured her. "Your mother and her new husband will be here, and surely your cousins are coming up from New York."

"Oh, Stanley," there was genuine distress in her voice. "I don't mean family. I know they'll be here. But that's just a handful of people. Will anyone else come? I don't know if Uncle Bennie had any friends." She looked around at the rows of empty pews.

Stanley couldn't tell if she thought a sparse showing would be an embarrassment to her or a disappointment to Uncle Bennie. He thought he should put his arm around his wife's shoulder, but he was distracted by an odd notion that entered his head. If this were his funeral, he realized, he didn't much care who would be in attendance. The idea of his children, his wife, his friends stopping by for a final good-bye struck him as rather unnecessary. And the measuring of a man's worth by the counting of heads at his funeral left him as cold as Bennie was now.

Nevertheless he was relieved, not for himself but for Mary Ann, when people began arriving. They came in twos and threes at first, then began coming in waves, undulating into the cathedral, winding their way through the pews, talking softly to one another, occasionally wiping a tear.

Mary Ann was more flustered by the crowd than she had been by the emptiness, and again Stanley couldn't be sure if she was pleased by the grand turnout or confused by it.

"Who are all these people? I don't know any of them! Where did they come from?"

"I would guess that your Uncle Bennie was a pretty popular guy to have all these friends."

"Friends!" Mary Ann searched the crowd for familiar faces. "Nobody has this many friends."

"Of course they do, dear." Then, in an effort to comfort her, he added, "why, we do. Don't you think that we would have a crowd like this at our funeral?"

The moment the words came out of his mouth he realized how ridiculous they sounded. Our funeral. Was he suggesting they would die together in some terrible crash – a plane or maybe just in the Volvo, and they would then share a joint funeral? Mary Ann was too busy scanning the audience to notice this reference to their simultaneous deaths.

"That's different," she insisted. "We have jobs, a standing in the community, we belong to clubs. Naturally people would come. But Uncle Bennie never held a job for more than a few months, he didn't belong to anything. He was always off somewhere. How did he get all these friends?"

Fortunately the service was beginning and Stanley didn't have to ponder the implications of his wife's questions. In any case, he didn't really care. He was only interested in his own connection with Bennie, which had very little to do with their earthly relationship. It was the idea of Bennie to which he felt attached. He could only remember actually seeing the man a few times every couple of years, and none of them were particularly significant. Uncle Bennie was not known for showing up at organized occasions like holidays or weddings. But now as Stanley sat listening to the priest say mass, he realized that his encounters with Bennie were indeed significant.

A quick visit with him at La Guardia Airport came into Stanley's memory. It was just the three of them. A vivid picture of Mary Ann's face that night came to him. Her hair, long and curly, bouncing against her shoulders when she laughed, and she laughed so much that night. Uncle Bennie had just returned from England and they had met him for dinner at the airport. Bennie was doing an impression of the Queen telling little Prince Charles the facts of life. Then Mary Ann had taken her shot at doing the Queen. She wrinkled up her nose, pursed her lips trying to look upper class, and out came the most terrible cockney accent. The laughter – that's what he remembered most. Stanley looked at the woman sitting next to him in the pew and he thought perhaps it was that night, twenty years ago, watching her laugh, that had kept him with her.

When the service ended Stanley realized he had barely heard a word that was said. He just caught the last few instructions. The congregation was told the hearse that would be carrying the casket would leave from the rear of the cathedral and they were invited to follow it to the cemetery for burial.

People began to leave. Stanley took his wife's arm, guiding her through the crowd. Once outside he was not surprised to see that the sky had turned a menacing steel gray. A drop or two of rain touched his face. Mary Ann felt the drizzle and looked at him as if waiting for a comment on his correct forecast, but instead he put his arm around her shoulder and hurried her to the car.

They drove around to the rear and joined the line of cars that would follow Bennie to the cemetery. As they wound through the streets the weather worsened. The drizzle turned to showers and then into a full scale downpour. The rain hit the windshield with such force that it was difficult for Stanley to see more than a few feet in front of the car.

"Is your mother going to the cemetery?" he asked, more to break the silence than because he cared one way or the other.

"No. She's having the immediate family over after, so she wanted to get home and prepare things. I can't get over that mass of people. I wonder if they'll all come to the burial."

She reached over, putting her hand on his arm. "I can't see a thing out there in this rain. Are you all right driving?"

"It's not that bad. I don't have to look for street signs or anything. I'm just following the car in front of me."

"I couldn't drive in this," she admitted patting his arm, and he knew, through the unspoken language they had learned to communicate in over the years, what she meant. The statement and the gesture taken together said thank you for being here, thank you for being in charge.

"We'll be all right."

"Do you know where we're going?"

He glanced at her to see if he could detect any subtext of disapproval in her face. Would she be angry if he said no? He took a risk.

"I haven't got a clue," he said with an exaggerated British accent.

He was relieved that she didn't rail at him for not having directions and that his thin attempt at humor had actually brought the tiniest hint of a smile to the corners of her mouth.

An inordinate amount of time was passing. Stanley began to wonder if the cemetery could be this far from the cathedral. Through the rain he could just barely see a traffic light turning red ahead of him. He managed to step on the brake just in time to avoid hitting the bumper of the car he was following. A moment later he was astonished by a knock on his window. He rolled it down several inches, shielding himself from the rain that came slicing in, hitting his face with razor sharpness. A heavy-set man in his late seventies, his coat held over his head, poked his broad nose through the crack in the window.

"Excuse me, old chap, but I'm a bit confused," he said with a true British accent. "Shouldn't we have taken a left at the bridge? I may be all turned about in this rain, but it seems to me we should be going west, not east about now."

"I'm just following the line," Stanley said. "But on that last turn I think I saw the hearse up ahead."

"Well, I'm sure you must be right. Wouldn't want to lose him, you know. As long as we're still following Bennie." The man hurried back to his own car as the light changed to green. Stanley rolled up the window and looked at his wife. "Do you suppose that was one of Bennie's cronies from England?"

"He sounded more authentic than you did. Did you really see the hearse?"

"Yes, I think so." The traffic began to move. "It's not like we could be lost. We're an official part of the funeral party."

"Maybe the whole party is lost," Mary Ann said. "The driver of the hearse could be leading us anywhere."

The idea appealed to Stanley. He imagined an endless line of cars following a long black hearse. The camera would focus in on the lead car — the hearse — the driver a zany Peter Sellers type character with one hand on the wheel and the other fanatically untangling a shredded map. At the last moment the driver decides to go right at the bridge. The swift turn swings the coffin against the wall of the car, the lid pops open. But instead of a body inside, there are boxes of brilliant diamonds. The driver speeds on. The camera closes in on his face, the face of a young Uncle Bennie.

The fantasy made Stanley want to laugh out loud. He had a sudden urge to share the image with Mary Ann, but she was sitting stone-faced, staring out the window. It wasn't, he thought, as if he and Mary Ann had become humorless over the years. They could both still enjoy a good comedy or a well-told joke, but the spontaneous laughter that was so much a part of their early relationship had long ago been suffocated by small arguments and the need to make so many daily decisions.

Another fifteen minutes passed and it was becoming undeniably clear to both of them that they could no longer be en route to the cemetery. Something was clearly wrong.

A few minutes later the line of cars came to an abrupt stop. In spite of the rain Stanley could see the outline of a large hotel. People were getting out of their cars, raising their umbrellas, wandering about, talking with each other. Stanley joined them. Mary Ann remained in the car.

"Where are we?" a short, round woman with puffy gray hair

asked. Her question was directed to no one in particular.

"Well, we're certainly not at the cemetery," came a reply through the rain.

"Isn't this the Lansford Hotel? What are we doing here?" another voice came from up the line.

Information went back and forth between the cars. It was becoming clear that the mistake had occurred at the Pikestaff Bridge over thirty minutes earlier. The first car in line, blinded by the rain, had turned right and crossed the bridge, mistakenly following a black limousine that looked like the hearse that was carrying Bennie. The limousine had then led its ribbon of followers to this hotel.

"Who is in the limo? Is it someone famous?" The random conversation was taking a new turn. "Somebody said it was a rock star."

"I heard it was Enrique Iglesias," came an enthusiastic voice.

"This is terrible," a woman squealed. "How are we ever going to find Bennie?"

"It's too late anyway. I'm sure they have him in the ground by now, what with this pouring rain and all."

"Well, I think it's fate. Bennie doesn't want us all standing about in the rain crying. I think we should go into the bar and have a good toast to him. That's what he would like."

Stanley got back into the Volvo looking puzzled.

"Well?" Mary Ann asked. "Don't just sit there. Tell me what's happening? Where are they all going?"

"To have a drink," Stanley replied, a tone of wonder in his voice.

"What are you talking about?"

Stanley explained the reason for their misguided journey and suggested they join the others in the bar.

"Are you insane? I'm not going in there. We don't even know any of those people. We'll go back to my mother's house. You do know how to get there from here, don't you?"

Sadly, Stanley turned the car around as they drove in silence to his mother-in-law's home. The dining room table displayed enough food for fifty people, but only eleven had arrived. Even with the small group, Mary Ann was busy sharing the hostess responsibility with her mother. There was much talk of who prepared what dish and little to no talk of Bennie. Stanley planted himself on a straight back chair next to a side table in the living room well away from the food conversation. He was handed a plate stacked with wild rice, arugula salad and jumbo shrimp.

Without taking a bite, Stanley picked up the plate and carried it into the kitchen, placed it on the counter and quietly called Saint Catherine's Cathedral. He then slipped out the back door and drove off in the Volvo. Twenty minutes later he pulled up at the cemetery, parked the Volvo and walked around back to open the trunk. He reached under the plaid blanket and took out the red umbrella. The rain had slowed to a gentle drizzle as he walked the muddy path between grave sites. The groundskeepers were just placing a temporary marker on Benjamin Jay Gladstone's grave.

Chairs were still set up around the site. Stanley took one and sat down next to Bennie.

"You had quite a turnout, Bennie. They seemed a good-natured group. I guess you had a lot of friends from England. I've never been there, you know. Wish I could have talked to them longer. How ever did you meet all those people?"

Stanley imagined how this moment would look from above.

A lone fellow sitting under a red umbrella talking to a dead man. The single red umbrella would suggest that the film was going to be a comedy, not a tragedy. It would beg the camera to zoom in on the face under the bright canopy. It would be his life that would take over the film, leaving the man in the casket as prologue, or backstory.

Stanley Watersmith. This would be *his* story.

Little Lies and Serious Indiscretions

Lyle had trouble holding on to things – his keys, his wallet, his wives, his morals, his ethics. Sitting in the defendant's chair in a downtown criminal court room, Lyle's mind wandered. Where had he gone wrong? He was a fifty-eight year old man, at least sixty pound to the right of optimum, and now with a rapidly disintegrating fourth marriage. His lawyer was standing before the jury giving his closing argument – pleading Lyle's case with rather unusual tactics.

"Ladies and Gentlemen of the jury, I ask you to consider the testimony you have heard over the last two weeks. I have no doubt that you have been given little reason to trust the business abilities of my client. I myself have to admit that there is no point in my standing here and defending my client's competence. We have heard extensive testimony from his current wife and three ex-wives as to his, shall we say, lack of attention to details. His business colleagues agreed that the defendant was not careful with facts or information."

It was true, Lyle thought: looking for his lost bits and pieces occupied great chunks of his time. He recalled an early morning walk along the wide Santa Monica beach last summer. He had removed his Rolex watch, a gift from wife number four, hiding it in a paper bag containing half of yesterday's ham and cheese and left it on the floor of the car's back seat. He had congratulated himself on his cleverness; what thief would bother looking in a dirty, smashed paper bag. Later that day Lyle had taken his car to be washed and waxed. He kept the Newsweek and the old coffee mug but the rest of the junk on the floor he tossed into the garbage bins. That night between the stir-fried rice and the moo goo gai pan, Lyle had remembered the Rolex. His late night search through the trash at the car wash was fruitless. The bins were deposited at five p.m. nightly into great dumpsters that defeated Lyle's determination to retrieve the watch.

Two options remained open to him; he could either tell his wife that he had been mugged while walking on the beach or he could replace the gift at great personal expense. The choice was obvious. Spending money gave Lyle a headache, and making up stories was always a challenge. The mugger's face formed itself in his imagination as he drove home that night.

Elizabeth, wife number four, didn't buy the story. After all, she had been with Lyle just the week before when he had placed his wallet on top of the car while he searched his pants pockets for his keys, then, finding them, jumped into the driver's seat and took off letting his wallet fly into oblivion. Then there was the time he had put their $120 opening night theater tickets in his shoe for safekeeping, remembering their whereabouts on the Sunday morning after the performance.

* * * * *

Why had it been so difficult to hold on to things, he thought. The women swam in front of him with their first sweet words and their lovely early scents, one for each decade of his adult life. Katie, in his twenties, married him for his careless innocence and divorced him for his equally careless betrayal. Andrea, in his thirties, married him for his rugged good looks and divorced him when rugged turned ragged. Wife number three, Erica, married him in his forties for his impressive legal career and divorced him for the even more impressive illegal gardener. The present Mrs. Dillard had married him in his fifties for his money and now she was leaving with it.

The desperate voice of his attorney pulled Lyle back into the present.

"I would never stand before this jury and insult your intelligence by saying that Lyle Dillard is a trustworthy individual or that he is a man of strong character; but is he a man capable of the intentional tax fraud that he is accused of in this courtroom today?"

Nausea tickled the back of Lyle's throat. His defense seemed more damning than the charges against him. The jury could only acquit him if they believed he was a walking case of benign neglect, a stupid but harmless bumbler only capable of committing unintentional fraud with no malice aforethought, in fact no forethought whatsoever.

Lyle, full of self-pity, had to face it. He was a light-weight kind of a guy. Things just floated away from him. He was a man not to be taken seriously. And after all he was guilty. He had intentionally doctored the books to hide over half-a-million dollars in income. He was no fool, he thought, as he heard his lawyer recall the time he had accidentally shown his accountant the wrong books which were in fact the right books.

As the members of the jury listened to his lawyer's closing remarks, Lyle saw how they glanced at him with a confusing mixture of contempt and pity in their eyes. Lyle's mind wandered again as the judge give his final instructions to the jury and sent them off to decide his fate. It took them only an hour to deliberate.

Lyle felt his lawyer's hand on his shoulder. "The jury is back," he said. Lyle was suddenly eager to hear the verdict.

"Have you reached a verdict?" the judge asked.

"We have, your honor," replied the foreman.

"Would you please read your verdict to the court."

"We find the defendant, Lyle Dillard, guilty as charged."

Lyle was astonished. Guilty! He might do real jail time for tax fraud. Guilty! A broad smile spread slowly across his face. So there, he thought – this should prove that I am a man to be taken seriously after all.

The Gypsy Moon

T hey find me a seat right down in front where I can see everything. Fluttering around me with pillows, lap blankets and parasols, the whole family encloses me as swarming butterflies do an old but still fragrant rose.

"Is that seat alright for you, Grandmother?"

"It's a bit chilly. Can we get you a shawl, Meg?"

"They have tea up in the clubhouse. Why don't I get us all a cup?"

When you live as long as I have, you find everyone is hungry to wait upon you as if the most important thing in the world was that your old body be comfortable. They mean well with all that fussing, but they don't understand that the aches and pains of age are just a distraction now, like a mosquito buzzing around your ear at night. Many years ago I found the secret place just above the spine, deep inside the brain where you can carry comfort like a tiny purse that holds everything a woman needs. I figured that's what an old woman needs, a special spot where she can carry the little things like her memories and her peace.

"Leave Meg alone now. She's just fine. Everybody sit down. The show's about to start." My grandson's booming voice rises above all the others. I can always count on him to get everybody to calm down.

My hearing isn't so good anymore but I still have eyes as sharp as a hawk. Long years and good eyes run in the family. My mother lived to be ninety-eight and read the morning paper every day, front to back. At the end, she'd be telling people she was only mid-eighties and they'd believe her. I never could lie about my age—shave even a year or two away. They all know I was born at the century mark so my years are as plain as the calendar. We celebrated my ninety-third birthday last month at my granddaughter Nadia's home. Nobody knows what to give an old lady. What in God's name do they think I want with more china creamers, toast warmers and Wedgewood candy dishes?

The trumpets sound the call to attention. Not a cloud spoils the cool mid-summer sky as the opening ceremonies begin. The young ladies parade their mounts around the ring, showing off their grace and discipline. Cara stands out from all of them with her shining red hair in a single braid hanging to her waist and her black eyes, huge as a great horned owl's, flashing at the judges as she holds her horse to a slow metered prance. Sitting high on her black stallion, her long slim legs in tight riding pants is my Cara, my great grandchild already sixteen years old. Her thighs hug her mount just as my mother's did eighty-three years ago. I have twenty-three great grandchildren at the last count but Cara is special. Cara, named for my mother, Cararina – Cara.

The loudspeaker is strong enough even for me to hear. "Cara

Yalosky is riding Gypsy Moon, a two year-old stallion. This is Gypsy Moon's first Class A competition."

It is a dream to see Cara float over hedges and fences effortlessly.

As I watch her, I drift into the timeless world where memories become crisp like the crust of freshly baked bread. It is a thing that a body learns to do after it has walked upon this earth for over nine decades. I am a child of ten again. It is a hot summer morning. I am begging my father to let me ride like my brothers.

"How can you ask such a thing?" he says not in anger but genuine surprise. "A young lady doesn't put on pants like a man and spread her legs across a horse's back. There is a perfectly good saddle for you if you want to ride so badly."

"No," I pout. "That's a side saddle. I can't gallop on that saddle."

"You don't see your mother riding like a boy, now do you?"

There is no use arguing with him. My father's word is law in our house. I sulk off to the bam. It's true, my mother rarely rides our horses and when she does it is always in a long proper dress that exposes not even an ankle bone. Side-saddle she rides, her red hair pulled back into a tightly twirled bun with never so much as a strand out of place.

My mother is in the barn brushing the new spring ponies. I hear her before I see her — the soft sweet hum that she always makes when she works. It is never a song or a melody but just a sound like a cat purring. I watch her for a moment before she realizes I am there. Her hands gently move across the pony's back. How I envy her. She wears serenity like a fresh white apron that never needs laundering but can magically clean and renew itself each day. My own heart burns with passions that I can't begin to understand. I love our home, this vast Texas ranch my father has homesteaded for us, but there is a mystery that hides in me calling me to distant places across lands and seas. Sometimes I feel that if I stay here for the rest of my life, my spirit will have to rise up out of my body and travel through the sky to visit all the places I only know in books and photographs. I hunger to see everything, to do everything. As I watch my mother, I wish that I had been born with her peaceful ways.

Later that day my brothers and I play wildly upstairs.

"Cararina," I hear my father call my mother. "The children are raising the devil. I think you better look to it."

Noise is something my father doesn't believe in. There is a whole list of rules that define my father's private religion. He lives by these rules and demands that his family do the same. We are told his rules daily. "Never raise your voice inside the house and absolutely never raise your voice in anger to any man." Of course, I know when he says "any man" he means me and mother too. Mother doesn't question his rules but I know that she doesn't believe in them the way he does, because when he's out working in the field we can scream our heads off and she doesn't stop us.

But now, once he has spoken, she comes dashing upstairs.

"Shh, shh," she whispers. "Please children, you must keep your voices down or you'll disappoint your father."

Instead of scolding us, she makes-believe she is breaking imaginary eggs on the floor and leads us around as we all pretend to walk on the egg shells without letting out a peep. We share a silent laugh, our hands smashed over our mouths as mother hugs each of us in turn, putting the smooth skin of her beautiful face next to our cheeks. She leaves our playroom, carefully checking her hair to replace any fallen wisp, then straightens her dress and apron.

That night I am in bed unable to sleep in the damp mid-summer night's heat. The sky is almost as bright as day. A full moon hangs low in the sky, a great hovering globe of soft white light. Mother comes in as she does every night to tell me a bedtime story. Her stories don't come from the children's books my father buys for me every year at Christmas. She sits quietly for a few minutes at the side of my bed. Then the gleam comes into her eyes and I know a wonderful story with magical characters is about to fill my tiny attic bedroom.

"This is a tale about the moon," she begins. "During the summer solstice, on the day when the sun leaves the sky for the shortest time, the full moon doesn't cross high in the heavens as usual, but creeps low near the earth, afraid to offend the quickly returning sun. This special night happens only once a year. It is called the night of the Gypsy Moon because the moon hugs the earth, moving like a vagabond from town to town. The Mexican people say that on this night the moon sails so low that it actually touches the earth, and in that second it is transformed into the body of a beautiful woman dressed like a bride covered in white. She is called la mujer en la luna.

"When the thick clouds hang like a mist over the grasslands, this white woman floats across the country, whispering to the young girls as they sleep. She calls them from their dreams to follow her to a secret place hidden from the sun. The girl children who are brave enough, follow her to a secret place where the magic begins. The owls, the cougars, the horses, the eagles all come to see la mujer en la luna. They approach her timidly because they know how powerful she is. Then, just for one night, each young girl is allowed inside the body of the animal she chooses."

Lost in her own imagination my mother tells me the adventures the girls have as they live as creatures of the night. I fall asleep picturing myself with the wings of an eagle, looking down at our ranch from so many miles up that I can see the borders of our land.

At three a.m. I wake with the heat baking my small third floor bedroom. I go to the window to let in the night air. As I pull the white lace curtains to the side a slight movement, a shadow, catches the corner of my eye. It moves in the direction of the barn. At first I am frightened and think to wake my brother but the moon holds me mesmerized. I wait to see if the shadow will return. In a few moments it emerges from the barn leading one of our mares. As the figures cross into the light of the moon, I can see them clearly. It is a woman walking with the new mare my father named Lady Grace because, he said, she held a canter like a blue blood. The woman's red hair is loose and wild, hanging below her waist. She wears a white lace nightgown that reaches the ground. In a single gentle move, the woman pulls up the gown to reveal long naked thighs, and leaps upon the back of the mare. Holding the mane, she touches Lady Grace's flanks with her bare heels. They gallop off into the moon.

The woman is my mother. How spectacular she is to me with her red mane flying in the night. I have never seen her hair loose before. She looks like a gypsy and not my mother at all.

I wait by the window for over an hour until I see her long shadow walking beside the shadow of the mare. As they come closer, I can see that both their bodies are covered in sweat. They walk through the tall wheat grass, my mother's gown still tucked up to her thighs. When they are just under my window, my mother glances up and for a second our eyes lock. My heart beats frantically. I break from the window and race back to my bed. Scrambling between the sheets, I try to lie silent, stilling my breath.

I hear her footsteps as she moves through the hall towards their bedroom. Will she pull her night dress over long bare legs before she gets back into the big canopy bed with my father, or will the skin of her thighs lie naked next to him? My insides twist, tickling my belly. No matter how tightly I close my eyes, I can't stop seeing my mother's body, her legs so strong and beautiful. Does my father run his hands up those legs touching her in the night? Does her long red hair fall across his chest? Do they move together in the night like a woman and a horse under the moon? My eyes burn as I pinch them even tighter, trying to squeeze the pictures out of my mind.

Never once have I seen my father kiss my mother on the mouth. Last month, on her birthday, I remember he gave her a quick peck on the cheek like he gives me when I've helped mother bake a lemon cheese pie or something else especially good. But when they are alone it must be different. My brothers have told me things and I have seen the stallions and the mares in the fields. But somehow these things didn't seem to have anything to do with my parents until tonight. Sweat beads up on my chest. The hunger I felt in the barn this morning gnaws at my heart.

The next morning my mother quietly sits at breakfast, her hair pulled tightly back once again. We all clasp hands and wait. After a moment of silence my father says, "Bless you Lord for this good food and for all your mercies." My mother passes me a plate of warm blueberry biscuits. I can feel her eyes burning into me, forcing me to look at her. When I do, she smiles and gives me a knowing wink. I flush hot all over my body, embarrassed to know her secret. The smile vanishes from her face as she sees my shame. The eyes that have never looked upon me with anything but love seem to narrow. Her familiar serene face has disappeared leaving tiny taut lines around h6r mouth. An invisible power holds my eyes to hers. In that brief second my world cracks into a chaos of unrecognizable pieces. My mother has allowed me to see inside her soul, and she is not the woman of quiet ways that I had envied. We share the same hungry blood. I don't know whether she has given me a gift or a curse, but in this brief moment my destiny has been dramatically altered and nothing will ever be the same again. Her kind hard eyes have given me permission. A chill touches my spine as I see the future and know with certainty that her choices will not be my choices. Then just as quickly the sweet mother face returns. We all eat breakfast as if nothing has happened.

* * *

It is strange how the past and the present become all mixed up when you get old. My mind floats like a leaf in a slow moving stream. Sometimes it gets caught on a twig or a rock and stops for a while as the water moves around it. Or maybe it defies the current and sneaks upstream in a back eddy. Time isn't as straight a line as most people think. I can close my eyes and eighty-three years melt like so much April snow in the afternoon sun. Then suddenly, I'm back again inside this tough weathered skin, watching my great granddaughter fly like an angel on the back of a mighty horse.

Cara came to visit me two years ago when her parents told her the black colt would be hers. She wanted me to give her foal a name. For almost a century I have been the one to name every new foal. It was late in June and my mother's story of the Gypsy Moon echoed in my breast as it did every year around the summer solstice. I told the story to Cara that night. She listened as intently as I had as a child. "That's it," she said when I had finished. "We'll call him Gypsy Moon but I won't let him stay close to the ground. I'll teach him to be a jumper, to fly over walls and fences."

Cara was only fourteen years old but she burned with ambition. She came to me to share her plans because I was the one who promised that her dreams were all within her power. An old woman can be a powerful force on a young girl if she sets her mind to it. And it was in her blood all right, the passion for horses.

The passion had traveled for one hundred years from my mother. For my father the ranch had been a business and a pretty respectable one. But for my mother it was a love affair. When each new foal was born she would cry as she watched the wet, clumsy baby find its four legs and stand for the first time. Where she saw new life, he saw profits. The passion. It flows downstream through the female line, moving with the pulse of the current into the future.

The loudspeaker brings me back to the present.

"Cara Yalosky takes second place."

The family all around me breaks into applause. Cara comes racing over to share her joy with us. She hugs her mother and father then kneels to greet me. "Look, Great Grandma, the red ribbon."

I put my hand against her cheek, still moist from her ride. "You are magnificent," I tell her. She takes my hands in her own and kisses them.

Cara pops to her feet, undoing her braid and laughing excitedly. Her long hair breaks free and I see my mother, Cararina, dance before me.

Charlotte Corday

Lisa gently rubs aloe vera lotion into Ian's water-damaged legs. He moans in pain at the softest caress. Ian's skin is shriveling up. The constant itching and the red swollen cracks that run the full length of his legs take the glamour out of being this year's biggest star on Broadway.

Every night, except for Mondays when the theater is dark, Ian sits in a huge brass bathtub placed center stage like a kings' throne. For six months now he is the infamous Jean Paul Marat, electrifying audiences with his passionate political ping-pong with the Marquise de Sade. The play, a revival of the popular sixties drama, depicts the depraved guts of the French revolution. Critics were wildly applauding it as a mirror of today with the disgust for corruption and the ever widening gap between rich and poor. Tickets are being scalped at the door for four hundred dollars. The cast has just received notice that they are extended for another six months.

"I've got to get out of the contract," Ian groans. "My body can't take six more months in that damn tub. I don't know why the hell it has to be so realistic. Half the audience can't even see that I'm sitting in real water."

"But the other half can," Lisa replies. "Besides, the whole play is about suffering. They've got to see you, the leader of the revolution, trapped in a tub of cool water because you suffer from a skin disease. You're a metaphor."

"Well, I'm sick of being a fucking metaphor. Six more months! Christ. With this hit behind me I could be out in Hollywood making some real money."

Lisa hates when Ian talks like this. They had both been struggling actors with no grand credits to their names when they were cast in The Assassination and Persecution of Jean-Paul Marat by the Inmates of the Insane Asylum of Charenton, better known as Marat Sade. It was their first big break.

Eight months ago when rehearsals began, Lisa had walked around in a daze, intoxicated with life. "The lead!" She had written her mother. "I have the leading role...well, the leading female role, that is." Her part was decisively smaller than three others, all male. But she was Charlotte Corday! The secret betrayer of Marat, the assassin. The greatest moment in the play belonged to her as she came to Marat in his bath and plunged a knife through his heart. She was the climax, the triumph of the poor over years of debate and endless waiting for justice. She was action, swift and deep, stabbing into the soul of the poison.

Slowly Lisa had eaten her way into Charlotte Corday, this beautiful young woman chosen to seduce and kill. She practiced how Corday moved in her long dresses, through the streets of 18th century France. She imagined what Corday felt, what she thought about. It was a wonderfully complex role. Not only was she Charlotte Corday, she was an inmate in an insane asylum who was playing Corday. A play within a play. Lisa conjured up fantasies that would dance just beneath the surface in this crazy woman's confused mind.

The week before opening night Lisa had stood nude in front of the full length mirror examining herself. Thin, perfectly thin she thought proudly, running her hands up her narrow thighs. What was it they said in Vogue, or was it Glamour…when a woman was standing with her feet together, you should be able to see at least an inch of space between her legs just at the top so that the triangle of her erotic center was clearly defined? Lisa pressed two fingers into the inner thigh gap. Perfect. She was perfect for Charlotte Corday. Perhaps her body was part of the reason she had been picked for the role. Today her body was fashionable. You couldn't be too thin. But in 18th century France, Lisa knew her body would have betrayed malnutrition, a member of the lower class suffering from the years of lean before the revolution sucked the fat from the overfed aristocracy.

Lisa had learned to ignore the cramping in her stomach when it longed to be full and churning. The method actors were her idols. They didn't just play the parts, they became the people...put real flesh and blood on their bones. Robert DeNiro had gained fifty pounds to do Raging Bull, gone to insane asylums to prepare for the role in Awakenings. Although Lisa was five feet eight and a mere one hundred and fifteen when she was cast in Marat Sade, now at the approach of opening, she had dropped to barely over one hundred pounds.

It was in the last week of rehearsal that the stakes went up even higher. Lisa had started seeing Ian. She couldn't really call it dating as there was never any time for the usual stuff — long dinners, movies, walks in the park. They grabbed a pizza, ran lines for each other, and made love. She was the leading lady sleeping with the leading man! Every morning she woke feeling her dream begin again as heat slipped up the back of her throat rising into her mouth. Life was a rich chocolate éclair full of cream and fifty feet long.

The night of the first full dress rehearsal—costumes, make-up, most of the scenery in place—Lisa sat at her dressing table methodically placing in front of her on all the cosmetics that would transform her into Charlotte Corday. She was eager to meet Corday—to see her face-to- face. Still naked, she ran her hands up to hold her breasts, now only a touch of soft flesh surrounding hard nipples. Then, slowly she moved her hands down feeling Corday's sharp ribs jutting out against transparent white skin.

She began with her hands. Smooth, graceful and tan, the hands of a healthy young woman. She sponged on a chalky pancake base, then traced the veins with blue eye-liner. She filled in the natural indentations of her knuckles until they appeared puffy. Stretching her hands, with fingers taut and splayed, she stared at them as she knew the audience would when those hands held the long knife high above Marat's bare chest. Then with these sick, undernour-ished hands, she began to work on her face. First a pale pink base coat, then a rust to darken and sink the area below her eyes. After molding the face for twenty minutes, Lisa examined her reflection. The gaunt face of Charlotte looked back at her.

She was ten minutes late to the rehearsal. No one was pleased including Ian who was never a second late. The director made a rude remark embarrassing her in front of the whole cast. "We are not making children's theater here, young lady. You start earlier with the make-up if it takes you so long."

But Ian was kind later on. During a five minute break he kissed her on the cheek teasing her with Woody Allen's words. "Ninety percent of success is just showing up on time." He squeezed her tiny rear pushing his fingers into her flesh like he did when he made love to her. His lust for her was there all the time, like a hunger always waiting to be fed. She delighted in the power she had over him. It was a tangible thing that could be touched and tasted. Whenever she got close to him during a scene, she could feel the heat coming at her from his body.

But now after a six month run, Ian is bored with the play, ready to move on. Maybe even bored with her. They lie in bed motionless after exhausting each other. The remains of a pepperoni pizza are tossed on the floor. Lisa moves her fingers softly across Ian's chest, one of the few areas of his body free from the ravages of nightly soaking.

"The show's getting sloppy," he says, his mind now distant from the driving sex that had consumed it only moments ago. "My spotlight was a foot off its mark in the stabbing scene tonight. Mike is sitting up there reading a book through the whole damn play. He's missing half of his lighting cues."

Lisa's body still feels wet and sticky. She doesn't understand how Ian can disengage so fast. But she knows if she brings it up, it will start another argument. To keep him, she knows she has to stay on his ground, be his trusted friend when he is pissed off so that the anger will not be directed at her.

"You were great tonight—three curtain calls."

"So who gives a shit. I want out. Damn agent can't get me out of the simplest contract."

"Can I get you some more wine?" Lisa says in the soft thin voice of Charlotte Corday. It was seeping into her—the voice. Especially when she was in bed with Ian and he was being so unreasonable. The voice kept her calm when what she really felt was rage. He was the toast of the town—up for a Tony. His career was launched. He had everything, including her, and all he wanted to do was move on.

"Stop it!" he yelled, turning on her. "I hate when you use that simpy Corday voice. This stupid role is driving you crazy. It's a little cameo for Christ sakes. You're making a whole life out of it."

Lisa pays no attention to his nasty remarks. She is puzzled by something he said a moment ago. "Ian, how do you know where the lights are in the stabbing scene? I'm standing over you. You're always looking right at me with fear burning in your eyes, not at Mike or the spots."

"I'm an actor for Christ's sake. I've done this play a thousand times. I can do it in my sleep. I look right through you. I always notice the lighting. It's more important than anything else. It makes the play."

Lisa stops listening when he says I look right through you. The words are a blow. That is their moment together. Marat and Corday's eyes lock and in the same second they both know the truth, she has summoned the courage to kill him and he sees he is about to die. The audience feels the power of the moment. No one breathes. Time stops. She can hold the blade in the air as long as she wants. Everyone is mesmerized. And Ian, all he can do is wait, wait for her to plunge the prop knife into his chest. The knife whose soft rubber blade easily retracts into the handle. The knife with the small prop blood sack that pops open with the thrust, leaving a trail of red dye leaking from the wound.

And when this happens night after night, Ian looks right through her to see if the spotlight is hitting its mark. Lisa slips out of bed and returns with the bottle of white wine that sits on the dresser. She fills his glass.

"Thanks, baby." He drinks the wine and drops his head on to the pillow. She watches him as he falls to sleep. She looks at his nude body. His legs swollen, cracked, rotting.

The alarm wakes them both at ten a.m. Ian slams his fist down on the clock to stop the blurring noise. Then as always he reaches over to Lisa. Ever since he learned that the play was to be extended and he was trapped for another six months, he has woken up with a hard-on and he wants sex before anything else, before he could think or consider starting the day. At first Lisa had been flattered. She thought he desired her so much that possessing her was the first thing he thought about upon waking. But this morning when his hand grabbed her breast and he pushed himself on top of her, she knows that it is an erection born of anger and not desire. When he moans, his face inches from hers, she knows that he is looking right through her.

After the sex, Ian is immediately starving. He gives Lisa a dismissive little pat on her behind. "Go make us some breakfast."

The kitchen is a safe place. Lisa takes out a large bowl and begins to gather the ingredients that she needs to make a bread pudding. When she first got the role of Corday, she had bought a cookbook with wonderful 18th Century French dishes. She prepared them with wooden spoons and old-fashion mixing tools to put her in the mood.

Ian eats her rich food full of cream, eggs and butter without really tasting them. It could be anything stuffing his mouth while his mind is full of visions of the big screen. Lisa stands at the window of his tiny Upper West Side apartment, watching Ian eat.

"It's a sunny day. Maybe we could take a walk in the park." she says timidly, trying to keep Corday's voice out of her own.

"You go for a walk. I got stuff to do."

"What stuff? You're out all day. What stuff are you doing?"

"I'm working on getting my career moving. You think you do one successful role and sit back and wait for things to happen? You got to make them happen. That's what's wrong with you. You have no ambition, no drive. What the hell do you do all day?"

Ian had no interest in knowing the answer to his question. He was already gathering resumes, actors photos, and demo tapes. In a few minutes he would be out the door.

What does she do all day Lisa thinks. Her life had seemed so simple since she had moved in with Ian. They rarely got out of bed until noon until last week when news of the plays extension motivated Ian into this frenzy of self-promotion. She would spend much of the day in the kitchen cooking, baking, playing with her 18th century kitchen toys. Then maybe a shopping trip—a hat down in the Village, a purse in Soho. The money from the play wasn't great but there was enough to splurge on impulse purchases, a luxury Lisa had never before had. Then an early dinner and a seven p.m. call at the theater. It was the perfect day.

Just as Ian is about to walk out the door the phone rings. He drops everything dashing to pick it up. Lisa hears the excitement in his voice. She goes into the living room to listen to his end of the conversation.

"You're kidding! That's unbelievable. When does it start? Of course, no problem. A week to tie up loose ends? Hey, I can get my ends tied up in an hour if you want. OK, next Friday. Hey Frank, you're terrific!"

When he hangs up, Ian is a new man.

"A producer at CBS saw the play. He thinks I'm perfect for a new pilot they're doing for the fall. Can you believe it, they bought out my contract. As of Sunday night Peter moves into the bathtub. He'll be ecstatic—my understudy for six months and I never missed a performance. I'm free! Marat can rot without me."

Ian grabs Lisa, picks her up in his arms and swings her around. When he puts her down she feels slightly nauseated and dizzy.

"It's great, Ian," is all she can think of to say.

"You don't sound very happy for me."

"Well, it's just that...well, what about us? It's happening so fast... you're just going to leave?"

"Hey, you're only stuck for six more months. When it's over, get a ticket to Los Angeles and we'll see what happens."

* * * * *

Lisa walks down Columbus Avenue without any purpose or destination in mind. She stops at a flower shop and buys herself a dozen white roses, then carries them out in her arms as if she is cradling a baby. Her next stop is a gourmet cutlery shop. There are lovely carving sets all around her and lots of knives—all shapes and sizes—even one that looks amazingly like the prop knife in the play. The clerk tells her it sells for $89, a lot of money for one knife, but spontaneous purchases are fun.

That night Lisa goes to the theater early so that she will have time alone in the dressing room before the cast arrives. She goes through her now well-practiced ritual of creating Charlotte Corday. Her costume is a long white dress with layers of fabric that provide wonderful hiding places. The prop knife fits easily beneath the loose scarf tied at her waist. There is plenty of room, enough even for her to place the new knife just alongside the prop knife.

Ian arrives late for the first time in the whole run. He doesn't even have time to say hello to Lisa before the stage manager calls a five minute warning. He must have been busy tying up loose ends, Lisa thinks. She is a loose end that can probably wait until the end of the week.

The house is full, the play is going perfectly. Lisa is patient. She avoids Ian during the first and second act intermissions. It is the third act that she is waiting for.

"Marat, it is the woman Corday. She wishes to see you."

"Let her in."

Charlotte Corday crosses the stage slowly, staring blankly at the people around her. She approaches Marat in his bath.

"Marat, the people are dying as you lie in your bath. Marat, I will tell you the names of my heroes but I am not betraying them, for I am speaking to a dead man."

The audience collectively holds their breath as they see Charlotte Corday slip a knife out from under her dress. She turns swiftly and faces Marat, the knife clasped with both hands over her head.

Ian sees that the spotlight is right on its mark but something is different. The light reflects off the blade. Steel not rubber. He stares up at Lisa as his body begins to tremble uncontrollably. He tries to speak but no sound comes to his throat. She stands over him for an eternity of seconds.

Lisa allows a tiny smile to touch the corners of her mouth. Ian looks terrified. But then he always looked terrified when she pulls the knife. He even trembles just as he is doing now. She has to give it to him, he is one hell of an actor.

"You have to die, Marat, the revolution must go on without you."

He can't hear her words anymore. She is saying things, lines not in the play. For a second she lowers the knife back down to her waist as if Corday has lost her courage. Ian manages to exhale. This is all a joke. Then her hands reach under her garment once again, the knife reappears and positions itself over his heart. With a powerful thrust Corday buries it in his chest. Ian collapses.

The play continues as the Marquis de Sade comments on the impact of Marat's death. There is thunderous applause at the final curtain. But to the audience's surprise the cast does not appear for a curtain call. The house lights come on quickly, signaling that the play is over.

Lisa sits at her dressing table, slowly removing her make-up. There is much noise and commotion backstage. It seems that Ian has passed out. Everyone is racing to get ice packs and smelling salts to revive him. The stage manager is calling 911. In a few moments Ian comes around. He is babbling about Lisa actually stabbing him with a real knife. He can't get the idea out of his mind, even after everyone shows him there is no wound anywhere on his chest.

Lisa puts her things into her large new purse. Among the tins of make-up she slides the long, sleek knife bought at the cutlery shop earlier that day. The night air chills her skin as she walks out the backstage door.

Safe Light

I first saw her in a Bleeker Street bookstore on Friday night. Her body was an unearthly blend of beauty and deformity. Customers stopped browsing and watched her move down the aisles, hiding their eyes. Hair, black and wild as a storm, framed her ash-white face. Sharp cheek bones lay behind skin that appeared to have no substance or depth. It was a porcelain face with wide unblinking eyes. Her left side was weak and fragile while the right side carried her weight. She walked carefully, tilting slightly to the strong side. From behind, her baggy sweater defined a curved back with a thickening on her right shoulder.

The shop owner, a man in his late seventies, nodded to the woman. I decided to ask him about her. I guess I seemed harmless enough because he talked to me.

"Her name's Grace. She's a weird one—been coming in here for years, always at night."

"What's wrong with her? I mean her body—her face."

"Polio is my guess. One night she bought a book on Jonas Salk.

I told her my brother's kid had polio in the fifties. She said nothing but that's what I think happened to her."

"I'm an artist," I said. "I'd love to paint her."

"You can forget that," he replied. "She doesn't like when people stare at her. Mostly she calls before she comes here and asks me to tell her if a book she wants is in stock. If we got it, I tell her the price and hold it for her under the counter. I know she wants to get in and out of here as fast as possible."

He watched Grace as she moved down the aisles. Overgrown eyebrows hanging under his thickly magnified glasses blocked small dark eyes. They looked like spider's legs grasping a black olive. The old man was her sentinel making sure she had safe passage on his land.

She was the right age for polio, about mid-forties. I guessed that the inactivity imposed by an iron lung had sculpted her child's body. The small muscles that structure a face had atrophied leaving her with a perfect child/woman mask.

A kid in the horror section looked away from a Stephen King book he was reading when Grace passed him. I saw his eyes follow her hands as she reached for a Chinese art book. Like a character in a No play, her left hand was the shadow of movement rather than the act itself. Just bone and skin, the hand removed the book in slow motion with great care. Aware of the boy's eyes, she averted her face and quickly went to have her purchase rung up. In a moment she would be out the door. I was desperate to meet her, to touch her, to paint her. A vision of her was already filling my canvas. Beauty so painfully housed. I searched for something to say to stop her from leaving.

"Excuse me," I blurted out. "I see you like 16th century Chinese art." She lowered her eyes and mumbled a sound of agreement. My mind went blank. Being this close to her, no words of response came to me. An eternity of seconds passed, then she turned and walked out the door. Without thought, I followed and quickly fell in step next to her.

"Mind if I walk along with you a ways? The name's Alan. I'm a painter. I do a lot of portraits—sort of abstracts...." I was babbling. She kept her eyes on the ground but did nothing to prevent me from walking beside her. My awkward attempts at casual conversation were a monologue of banality. Every few minutes she would nod her head and look vaguely as though she was listening. We had gone seven or eight blocks together, when she suddenly stopped. That incredible expanse of black hair lifted and she allowed me to see her eyes.

"Well, Alan," she said softly. "This is my loft. Would you like to come up for a drink?"

These were her first words in eight blocks. I was a stranger. For all she knew I could be dangerous. Why was she inviting me up to her place? This was New York City, for God sakes. Nobody asks a stranger in with such a quiet, innocent voice. I got that tingling sensation in my gut that I always get when I look down from a tall building—half fear, half this intense desire to jump.

I followed her into the converted warehouse. We climbed three flights of dark narrow stairs. Each step she took looked like a triumph over gravity as her right leg pushed her body forward. When we reached her loft, she removed keys from her purse and opened the door with that perfect slow motion hand.

"Did you forget to pay your light bill?" I teased her nervously. The room was lit only by candles. "Isn't it dangerous to leave these burning when you're not home?"

Without answering, she poured a dark red wine into crystal glasses and we sat on the hardwood floor. Sweat was accumulating on my back. I had to get her to talk.

"It's hard to get these great old lofts. Have you lived here long?"

"Ten years."

Her voice was strange, distant; my heart was racing with fear. Who was this woman? I kept talking. "Are you an artist—a painter or something?"

"I'm a photographer." Two sentences and she was already pouring herself another glass of wine. The candles cast striped shadows across the white walls. I was reminded of the old man's eyebrows. A spider's nest with the dark queen sipping red wine. Keep talking I thought.

"I'd really like to see your work."

She hesitated, then took me to her studio. "I don't know if you'll like my photography. It's kind of different." The walls were covered with her work. It only increased my sense of terror, but I didn't know why.

"These are incredible! I've never seen anything like this," I responded honestly. Then I realized where my fear had come from. All the photos had black backgrounds.

"What are you," I joked, "a vampire? These have all been shot at night."

It was a haunting collection of work. Men and women caught in nightlife poses on the streets of New York. But all of Grace's people were faceless—heads were turned away, bent, or in shadow.

"I'm glad you like them," she said in a flat indifferent voice.

One image was particularly overpowering. A woman in a

bright white cape, sitting on a narrow bed. Her knees were pulled in towards her body, held in place by exquisite hands. The cape opened slightly to reveal that she was nude under the huge expanse of cloth. One soft breast was visible.

"You should try to get a show. In a gallery. Your stuff is so unique. But what am I saying. Maybe you've had lots of shows." I was babbling again.

"Would you like to see my darkroom?" she said moving the black curtains that almost covered one wall. Behind them was a tiny room full of chemicals and developing trays. There were no candles in here, just the safe low darkroom lights. There was a single bed tucked in the corner.

The tingling sensation returned to my gut. The photograph that I had been admiring was shot in this room. "The woman on the bed," I said "It's a self-portrait, isn't it?"

"Yes," she said. "Sometimes I don't have anyone else to shoot."

I stared at the bed. "Do you sleep in here?"

"Oh, no. The bedroom is downstairs." As she spoke, she touched my arm with that fragile hand and drained the fear out of my body. I bent down to kiss her strangely beautiful face. Her lips parted softly. The faceless people in her photos left my memory. We made love in the single bed under the safe light. She allowed me to see her with my hands. I traced the twisted spine of her naked body with my fingertips. I could already see her erotic angles lying on my canvas.

"Do you do this all the time?" I asked.

"No, only when I need to."

"Then why me? I'm a perfect stranger."

"Oh, I don't think you are perfect," she said, "but you are

interesting."

Suddenly she jumped out of the bed and turned on a bank of bright overhead lights blinding me for a moment.

"Now you will pose for my camera," she said as if it were a demand and not a request. I felt the thin cover pulled away from my body leaving me naked under all that light. Then there were three quick flashes.

"No!" I shouted at her. "Stop. You have no right to photograph me like this." I felt the cold sweat return to my spine. "I mean, I am flattered and all, but...."

"Why did you follow me here?" she said accusingly. "Did you find me just too beautiful to resist?" Her sarcasm made my naked vulnerability even more intense. I couldn't see her; the spot lights poured into my eyes leaving her in shadow.

"Never made love to a freak before?" she said.

"No! I mean, you've got me all wrong. I wanted to paint you. I wasn't expecting this!" I said, indicating the bed.

In the now brightly lit room I saw photos that were hidden before. Photos of men lying naked in a corner with piercing flood lights casting their body parts in grotesque shadows. Shot in this room. Her collection from nightly hunts.

"Maybe I better leave," I said as I got up to find my clothes.

She grabbed my pants and shirt before I could reach them. "It's a trade," she said. "If you want my body, you have to give me yours."

In the same second I felt both sympathy and fear. She wanted to capture me, to have me be the victim when only a few hours ago in the bookstore, I had already sketched in my mind how I would capture her.

Out of the corner of my eye, I saw the white cape from her

self-portrait hanging on a hook next to the bed. In one motion I lunged for it, threw it around my naked body, and pushed pass her through the black curtains.

Stunned by my quick actions, she stood frozen. I ran through the living room to the door. I looked back as I left the loft. Only the darkroom lights remained on. In the soft red glow I saw her face, fierce and fragile. Her body was hidden behind the black curtains. The camera emerged in her white hands, pointed at me. Another series of flashes shocked me as I looked down, realizing the white cape had fallen open revealing my thin, nude body. Shame sickened me, knowing that I would now be pinned to her darkroom wall. She laughed softly. I turned and ran down the narrow stairs.

Neat as a Pin

Time was getting looser. Carol was used to a tight-fitting day. She lined up her chores and dutifully knocked them down one by one. Since her mother's illness, time lay in empty pockets. The stroke was mild but it would keep her mother in the hospital for at least two weeks. For now, no one was there to criticize her for not keeping her life in order.

Instead of straightening the house this morning, Carol roamed from room to room looking for something she had lost. She didn't remember what it was she was looking for, only that she had lost it. The search didn't reveal what she was looking for, but it did turn up her car keys, so she grabbed her purse and left the house. The daily tasks seemed unnecessary to her today. If no one came to visit, why pull up the bed covers just to pull them down again at night?

Carol drove aimlessly through the San Fernando Valley determined to take charge of her day, but just how to achieve this eluded her. Each time she felt on the verge of an idea, it slipped away before it could form itself in her mind. She watched the store fronts pass by. The lighting shop on Moorpark was full of crystal chandeliers sparkling in the afternoon sun. What an effort to dust, she thought, and the clarity of the thought surprised her. She had spent the last six years polishing and dusting her mother's house.

Ironically, a failed marriage had sent her back to the home she had married to get away from. At thirty-eight she had become the dutiful daughter once again. She listened politely to her mother's little speeches on how one should properly live one's life. As a child these miniature lessons were burned into her brain daily. They were the bible of mandatory "never rules" that governed a civilized life. "Never touch the dusty pews, you'll leave dirty marks on your white gloves. Never leave the house unless it is spotless from top to bottom."

I need something to do, she thought. The words were said out loud with such desperation that it frightened her. Something to keep her from going back home, at least for a while. She passed a gourmet meat market. In the past, she would have parked the car and reluctantly walked into the shop to chat with the butcher while considering at length what her mother would want her to make for dinner. What a waste of time, she thought.

She drove on. The pressure to find something to do found its way into her temples. They started to pound and leak pain into her eyes. Lights began to strobe in her peripheral vision. Oh, my God, another migraine aura. She had been getting them every few weeks now. This time it wasn't her brain creating the strobing. She was relieved to notice that the lights were coming from a colored ball twirling in front of a sign advertising Yvette, the Amazing Fortune Teller. She vaguely remembered seeing it here before. It looked out of place sitting on a main boulevard in the middle of all these serious merchants. It belonged off a side road in a some small poor town. "Tarot Card Readings," the sign read. "Guidance for your Future."

What crap, she thought, but her right foot slowly eased off the gas pedal. A parking spot opened. It's something to do, she excused herself. She passed the strobing ball quickly hoping no one would see her. "Ring here," a badly painted sign pointed to a pull string bell. If she's really psychic, she knows I am standing here and I shouldn't have to ring the stupid bell. She pulled the string. A brassy note sang loudly, embarrassing Carol. There was still the possibility of a fast retreat.

The door opened and she was face to face with a woman in her mid-fifties with perfect white skin and glossy black hair flying in all directions. The woman's face stared at her for a second, then broke into a toothy smile. "Welcome," she said, "come into my home."

Once through the door, Carol realized that the store front was just that, a front. It was built to make the old stucco house look legitimate. Yellow flowers peeled off the papered walls. Shelves coming off the hinges displayed hundreds of pictures in cheap plastic frames. Candles sat in soggy piles of wax and dust. Dolls made of dried-up fruits straddled a cracked conch shell and tacky romance novels. Carol was so disgusted that she wanted to leave, but that would be rude. I'll act interested, polite, and get out of here as fast as I can she thought. She tried to calm herself but her heart was racing.

"You look so frightened, my dear. My name is Yvette. Come and sit down."

Her voice was soft and comforting. Carol did what she was

told.

"Why have you come to see me, my child?" Yvette asked. Anger flashed across Carol's face. She was thirty-eight years old, hardly a child.

"Please don't be upset with me," Yvette begged. "I am only here to help you. Do you want to know what lies in your future?"

Her words were a gentle caress. Carol began to relax. "I don't know why I'm here," she said awkwardly. "Do you read my future in cards or something? How much does it cost?"

"Why don't we start off very slowly?" Yvette's voice was hypnotic. "We can talk a little first, get to know one another. Let's not worry about money. Why don't you just give me a token amount? Perhaps ten dollars."

It certainly was reasonable. Carol opened her purse, unfolded her wallet and searched for a ten dollar bill. Less than going to a movie. "What do we talk about?" she asked.

"Think of me as a friend. A friend with special knowledge about you. Give me your hand." Carol volunteered her hand. "You have a beautiful palm, but the lines are small and weak. You have lost something—a very important thing—and this frightens you."

Carol's face began to burn.

The tips of Yvette's fingers rubbed Carol's palm gently. "This thing has been lost for a long time, so long that you didn't even remember that it was gone. But now I feel the energy in your body changing. You want this lost thing back. I can help you, Carol, if you trust me."

Carol pulled her hand away in shock. How did this woman know her name!

"Listen to me," Yvette continued softly. "Go home and look

for what you have lost. You will know when you see it. Then come back to me. I'll be here."

Back in the safety of her car, Carol got on the freeway in rush hour traffic. The further she got from Yvette the more she felt the whole thing was foolish. She never intended to return to that dirty place. Her mother's voice hung in the air. "Neat as a pin," her mother was fond of saying. She wondered where that expression came from. How was a pin neat? It did seem appropriate though. Her mother's house was always neat as a pin. When she was ten, Carol remembered her Father saying, "It's a god damn palace. We should put up those little ropes you see in museums around the living room." He left for the last time the next day.

It was seven o'clock before she got home. The routine called for dinner at six. Now that her mother was ill, she was expected to call the hospital at exactly six.

"Why aren't you calling on time?" her mother demanded. "It's seven o'clock!"

"I'm so sorry, the traffic was terrible. I lost track of the time. There was a long line at the bank." She wanted to go on with a litany of apologies but her mother wasn't interested. "You haven't got anything to do all day. You could visit me or at least call me on time." The subject was dropped and her mother went on to complain about the sloppy staff on the evening shift.

Later that night Carol stared out her bedroom window at the ocean. Her mother was right, she didn't have anything to do all day. She hadn't had anything to do for six years. She searched her memory for things that she had done over the years. Nothing came to mind but housework, endless meals, and shopping. If someone stood looking through this window from the other side, she thought, they would see an empty room. Her life was so thin the full moon could not cast her image in the smallest shadow.

The whole of the next day she sat at the window waiting for something to move her. Nothing did. At five, she got up to make a cheese sandwich for dinner. At precisely six she phoned her mother. After three days of sitting, Carol began to feel different. She stopped waiting for something to move her. She was enjoying not moving, just thinking randomly. She was glad her mother and her "never rules" were out of the house. But she knew it wouldn't be for long. For most of her time at the window, she felt quiet and indifferent. When she did feel an emotion, it was fear.

At four o'clock on Friday, Carol remembered Yvette. She remembered her exact words. "Go home and look for what you have lost." Suddenly it was extremely important for her to see Yvette. After three days of sitting her legs were shocked by the rapid movement Carol demanded of them.

As she drove to the fortune teller's, she remembered how dirty the house had been. A feeling of nausea tickled the back of her throat, but her fear was stronger than the sick sensation. She realized that Yvette was right. She was terrified; terrified of not being perfect, terrified of making her mother angry. She was terrified of everything.

Yvette didn't seem at all surprised to see her. "Carol, my dear, come in. I knew you would be back soon. You haven't found it yet, have you? It's getting worse isn't it, this terrible fear?"

This woman is psychic, Carol thought, she seems to know me better than I do. The house was worse than her memory of it. Stale and filthy.

Yvette and Carol spent an hour together. "It's your turn, Carol.

It is time for you to take back your life. Your mother drinks the power from your veins. That's why the lines in your palm are so weak and thin. You must stop her from sucking away your power." Yvette's voice was mesmerizing.

Alone in the car again, Carol tried to think rationally about what Yvette had said. But she was too upset and confused for sane, logical thinking. Yvette was right. She had no power. She saw how her mother took it from her; how she treated her, always telling her what to do and how to do it. Yvette was right. But Yvette was strange. Her voice was sweet and gentle but Carol was afraid of her—of what she knew.

Every weekday for three weeks Carol went to see Yvette. Each morning she would decide never to return to the fortune teller again. By mid-afternoon the compulsion to go was so strong that she had no hope of fighting it. Her mother had returned home and was more demanding than ever. Carol kept her visits to Yvette a secret.

Each visit was the same. Yvette pushed her to take back her life, to destroy the people who sapped her power. Carol hated these visits. Yvette's house repulsed her with its dirt and neglect. Yvette insisted they have tea together at each session so that she could read the soggy leaves. The kitchen was the worst part of the small house. The counters were covered with paper cups, pizza boxes with moldy remains, and dishes left unwashed for weeks. The stove was caked with black burn stains and hardened food particles. None of the burners lighted properly to heat water -- the smell of leaky gas was the perfume of their little tea ceremony.

She could not stop going. The sessions with Yvette structured her day. Without them, she knew she would go back to sitting at the window and staring at the ocean. Carol did everything Yvette told her to do. She came home late, she didn't clean the house. Her mother was furious at the change in Carol's behavior. After weeks of raging at her daughter, she gave up and grew silent.

Yvette's words rung in Carol's ears consistently: "You must end this negative force in your life. Kill it before it stops you from finding what you have lost."

After three weeks of visits with the fortune teller, Carol had a dream that seemed so real she woke up in a cold sweat. A sweet-faced golden retriever jumped in bed with her. It reminded her of her best friend's dog when she was ten. She had begged her mother for a puppy right after her friend had gotten one, but her mother would not hear of it. "Never have pets in your house. They carry disease and filth." In the dream Carol was petting him and scratching behind his ears. Suddenly the dog morphed into a mangy, dirty mutt with her mother's face. It growled at her and snarled. As it lunged at her neck, she woke up. She heard Yvette's voice as if it was in the room: "Kill her before she kills you!"

Yvette

She woke up in a red velvet dress. For Yvette there was no distinction between her sleeping and waking wardrobe. She simply went to bed in whatever she was wearing. It was so much easier, she thought. That way you didn't have to get dressed in the morning. She changed clothes only when her mood changed.

Lately her mood was bright. She had a new toy to play with. A wonderful new toy, the best in years. Carol was the toy's name. She came every day, a piece of soft clay that Yvette knew she could shape any way she wanted. The minute Carol had walked through the door, Yvette knew this would be a gold mine. Carol fell for all her cheap tricks. She had opened her wallet to offer money immediately on her first visit giving Yvette plenty of time to catch a glance at a credit card. She had been so shocked when Yvette knew her name before she offered it. It was so easy manipulating her.

Yvette liked her work. After years of waitressing in small coffee shops, she had decided to start her own business. Being a fortune teller was the ideal choice. People had been ordering her around all her life. Now she could tell them what to do. Of course, she had to be subtle. She would use her predictions of their future to push them to act in the present. She would tell them to look for what they had lost. Everybody has lost something. Just these words sent people into desperate ill-defined fear. Naturally, she told them she would use her own special psychic abilities to help them find what they had lost. This intervention was expensive. Yvette never asked for high fees for her services but she did suggest her clients donate large amounts of money for candles and prayers to be lit and spoken on their behalf. Cash was stashed all over her house. Money was stuffed inside bedroom slippers, old sea shells, coat pockets. She liked getting the money. It represented the power she had over people, but she had little interest in spending it.

She hardly ever left her house. Her diet consisted of whatever could be delivered. That was the other wonderful thing about her work. People came to her—she never had to go out. No license was required for her work, so no one ever bothered her.

No advertising was necessary. People saw her strobing ball and walked in. Most of her clientele came three or four times, then disappeared. They either realized she didn't know much or they got bored. She knew that some left because they didn't like the look or smell of her home.

Carol was different. She came every day and did everything suggested. Yvette didn't even ask for candle money. The money didn't matter. The excitement came with the power she had over Carol. *The woman is so passive, insecure and frightened,* she thought, *she wants so desperately to please*—first her mother, and now me, Yvette thought.

When Carol told her how she spent her days, Yvette was full of loathing. She saw Carol as a useless non-person. Carol's fanatic cleanliness, her neat little outfits with Peter Pan collars and perfectly tied neck bows reminded Yvette of the snotty rich kids she had gone to school with. To them she was the tramp from the other side of the tracks, the outsider. She had lived alone with her mother in a shack that was literally across the railroad tracks from a well-manicured suburb full of children with pretensions. She watched them over the years as they planned their perfect futures. At fourteen her mother told her, "School is for rich kids. You quit and get a job."

Women like Carol didn't have to work at low paying jobs all their lives. Women like Carol were born in immaculate houses that stayed that way because their occupants had too much time on their hands and no imagination to help them use it. These women disgusted her with their empty lives.

Each day she speculated on just how far she could push Carol. She was obsessed with the desire to go as far as possible. If she could actually convince Carol that the only way to save herself and return power to her life was to get her mother out of her life permanently, Yvette would have her greatest achievement. She had never had a client capable of an actual violent act before, at least she didn't think so. Probably Carol wasn't able to commit such a crime either, but her personality was so weak and her will so malleable that maybe it was possible. And her mother was in such poor health anyway, it would be easy to give her a push.

An adrenaline rush made her fingers tingle just thinking about the possibility. She visualized her arms lengthening and reaching beyond her house to touch life outside. With Carol as her agent, she could cause a dramatic event. The idea was exhilarating. It consumed her days. The excitement kept her up until the early hours of the morning.

After two months of seeing Carol every day—she came even on the weekends now—Yvette felt she was ready for the ultimate suggestion. "You must remove the forces that are destroying your life. You must take the life of this person who has so much power over you or you will never be able to find what you have lost."

The seed was planted. Now, she thought, lying in bed in her yellow sequined evening dress, I just have to wait.

Carol

Movement returned to the house. Carol didn't sit at the window and stare out at the ocean any more. She got up early in the morning before her mother stirred, dressed quickly and left the house. She had things to do, things to learn. At 2:00 she always returned home to make the beds, clean the house, and prepare dinner.

They didn't talk much. Her mother ate silently, smiling occasionally. Carol thought she was simply grateful to have some order back in the house.

Purpose had come to her life. Her step was brisk. She had places to go. This morning her "to do" list had several items on it. The library was first. She hadn't been in a library since she was a child. It took her time to remember how to use the Dewy decimal system. But she was patient. She knew what she wanted. The Physicians Desk Reference, the PDR as the librarian called it, was where she got some of the information she needed. It listed thousands of drugs and explained their effects in detail.

Next was an appointment with a new doctor. She complained of chronic insomnia and he quickly offered her a prescription for Dalmane. She told him she had read that Halcion was better, much quicker acting. His pen scrawled out her request.

At noon she called her mother to say she had a special evening planned for her.

Then she went to Saks in Beverly Hills. This was the only place her mother ever shopped. But instead of going to the department that carried matronly dresses, Carol went to the lingerie department and bought a black silk nightgown cut excessively low in the back. She tucked the bag safely in the trunk and drove north through the canyon to the Valley. She had an appointment with Yvette at 3:00.

She passed the lighting store on Moorpark and stared at the lovely crystal chandeliers. When she reached the gourmet meat market, she parked the car. It was 2:30. She had time. The butcher made suggestions as to how different meats might be prepared. Carol took her time before selecting two thick filet mignon steaks.

She rang Yvette's bell at exactly 3:00. The door opened and Yvette's familiar voice greeted her.

If all goes well, thought Carol, this will be our last visit.

Yvette was excited and eager to know what Carol had planned. Carol said she was thirsty and suggested they have tea early today. "Oh, of course, my dear. I'll have it ready in a second." Yvette went off to the kitchen. Carol sat quietly looking around at the cluttered room. When Yvette returned with the tea, Carol said apologetically, "I didn't have time to stop for lunch. You wouldn't have just a cracker or something I could munch on?"

Once Yvette was back in the kitchen, Carol took out the little bottle with the six crushed Halcion tablets. She quickly stirred them into Yvette's hot tea.

They sipped their tea and talked for twenty minutes. Yvette's eyes began to droop and her speech was slurred. Carol waited patiently until Yvette's head slumped on the table. She had read that it could take up to an hour for a person to fall into a deep sleep state. She went into the bathroom and found some dirty towels. Once the towels were soaked in soapy water, she began her work. First she removed all the junk from the shelves. It all went into a large trash bag she had brought just for that purpose. Then she scrubbed the surfaces, removing years of dust and candle wax.

After an hour's time the shelves looked quite good she thought. Yvette was oblivious to all her hard work. She looked at her watch. It was 4:30. Time to go. She picked up her tea cup and went into the kitchen. She washed the cup and carefully wiped it clean. Then she located a potholder. With it she turned on the oven. She opened the oven door and blew out the flame. The usual smell of gas in the kitchen immediately worsened.

She picked up her purse and left Yvette's house. Once in the car, safely on her way home, she thought of Yvette's "never rules."

"You will never get your power back. You will never have control over your life." Carol smiled; at last she had found what she had lost.

Her mother would be proud of her: she had left Yvette's house as neat as a pin.

Putting Down Roots

A ndie bent over in her garden, breaking the darkness with the tiny beam of a flashlight. At 4 a.m. she was pulling weeds from between the sweet peas. Her thin body shivered in the chilly air. For two months insomnia had been slowly eating at her nights, taking small bites at first, then boldly devouring whole chunks like aphids preying on her roses. When the insomnia started, she was frightened. Disorientation closed around her each time she woke in the middle of the night. She lay alone for hours willing herself to sleep. But tonight when the insomnia came, she got out of bed and walked into the garden. Her fear disappeared as she worked in the silence. The night, she thought, had hidden the best hours from her, until now.

She pushed her fingers into the soil, damp with dew, carefully making sure that the entire root of the weed was dislodged so that nothing remained to steal the nutrients from the flowers. The roses were the most brilliant, with their rich yellow and red petals that shone in the moonlight. Andie loved them, not for their beauty, but for their proud independence. They waited on no one's approval, living only for themselves. She gently cupped her hands around the newest bud; its petals were the same color as her own blazing red hair. How she envied this flower's silent world... its freedom.

Andie lived alone in a tiny cottage behind a grand Coldwater Canyon estate in the hills of Los Angeles. Her one-room house had been the servant's quarters in better times. The current owners liked to rent out the cottage to young single girls who would be easy tenants.

The remains of an English garden grew wild just outside her door. The old couple in the main house cared nothing about its existence anymore—it had been left to its own will long ago. Tonight Andie sat inside the fenced garden and let its life fill her. She was quiet for so long that a broad-winged monarch butterfly found her finger tangled around a vine. It startled her. Hadn't it known that she was an alien...that she didn't belong in its domain? It stayed on her finger for several minutes before it took flight. Andie slowly stood, making her way back to the cottage.

It had been thrilling: the butterfly.

Back in bed, she dozed off peacefully.

At 7 a.m. the alarm clock woke her. She showered, dressed, and began the one-hour commute to work as a file clerk for an insurance company. Her gray VW Rabbit joined the long line of cars flowing down the canyon road to Sunset Boulevard. From there she drove west to the freeway. Her Rabbit crawled onto the ramp heading south towards Long Beach. She saw no passengers in the other cars, only a single mannequin driving each one. Lone suits, male or female, held in place with black stretched belts. A BMW sounded an angry horn and cut her off -- she thought she saw the car's bumper give her an evil grin. When she arrived at the huge Metro Life building that would encase her for the day, she wondered absently how she had gotten there.

The elevator took her to the fourteenth floor where she walked to a windowless cubby hole with stacks of files. The first thing she did was to take a small green pitcher out of her bottom desk drawer and go to the drinking fountain. She filled it with cool water, then returned to feed the thirsty philodendron and the Creeping Charlie on her desk. Carefully placed under a bright light, the plants grew daily and began to slip their curious leaves into the back of Andie's computer. She gently untangled the vines.

She opened the top file in the stack.

Tense from lack of sleep, Andie felt the office noise penetrating her body, jarring her spine and pressing against her temples. Phones screamed insistently, printers hammered page after page, people joked, laughing loudly. Andie ached for silence.

She had moved to Los Angeles from Manhattan two summers ago. Central Park in the spring, with its abundance of blooming color, had put the idea of California in her mind. She imagined it as a magical place where green was never covered by white and cold—a place beyond her mother's touch. It was her friend Sara's plan more than her own. Sara's uncle had gotten them jobs with a temporary agency doing office work. At the last minute Sara's mother wouldn't let her go. So Andie had come to Los Angeles alone.

Few co-workers talked with her during the day. At 2 p.m., Nancy, the department secretary, passed.

"Hey Andie, how are you doing? Your plants look great."

"Yes, they like each other," Andie stammered, wanting to say more but no words came to her.

"Well, I'll see you later." Nancy hurried off.

I make people nervous, Andie thought sadly. She often listened to conversations in the lunch room and marveled at how relaxed the people seemed with one another. She had tried memorizing pieces of random chat to use when she had an opportunity, but the right moment never came. When people spoke to her for more than a few minutes she would lose the meaning of their words, focusing only on their mouths opening and closing like fish freshly plucked out of water. The struggle to keep her mind on what people were saying—to stay aware—had gone on since she was a child. The effort to act like others, to hold together a simple conversation, was exhausting.

She had to try harder, she thought. She had to connect with people...make new friends. I can do it, she told herself, stirring up her courage. Instead of taking her afternoon break alone, she decided to go down the hall to the vending machine area where the fourteenth floor staff gathered. Just before she turned the corner to the break room she overheard words that froze her in place.

"God, she is so strange. She says things that don't make sense."

"I know," said a second voice. "She's talking to you one minute and then she's gone, like she suddenly hasn't a clue what's going on."

"Yesterday I had this terrible urge to snap my fingers right in front of her nose and say, you will wake up now and remember everything."

Their laughter spilled into the hallway.

Andie's eyes stung but she refused to let them fill with tears. She retreated to her cubby hole.

She sat at her desk staring into space. Her fingers tingled, heat burned her whole body...air moved through her skin. The feelings were familiar...she'd had them often growing up; they made her think of herself as different from other children. In her high school years she had managed to ignore the feelings, to make a few friends, even go to parties. But it was coming back...the loneliness and the fear. She ran her hands over the leaves of her cool moist plants.

At 4 p.m., Andie's mother called from New York.

"Andrea, dear, how are you? You know how I worry when you don't call. It's been weeks." She pronounced Andrea with an overly-accented second syllable, trying to give the impression of an upper class background. Andie had always hated the way her mother spoke her given name. Andrea. It sounded pretentious...phony.

"I'm sorry Mother. I haven't put a phone in my house and there never seems to be any time at work."

"Don't apologize in that whiny voice, dear."

"Sorry, Mother."

"How was your day? Are you getting any better sleep? Have you met any men? Are you going out?" The questions came in quick succession.

"Everything's all right, Mother." Andie searched her mind for words. She could feel her mother waiting for her to say more. It was difficult to catch her breath. She remembered the woman in the blue dress in front of her in the lunch line. Andie repeated the words she had overheard the blue dress say. "I just need a change, that's all. I want to quit this job and do something else."

"Oh Andrea, please!" a deep tone took over. "You've had five jobs in the last two years. Every time you quit, you lose your benefits, your chance for promotion and everything. You have to stop behaving like a child. You're twenty-four years old. You've got to start putting down roots."

Andie gently fingered the vines of the Creeping Charlie as her mother spoke.

She envisioned her mother, dressed in an expensive tweed from Bergdorf's, sitting at her grand mahogany desk—not a mother really, but Mrs. Jonathan Erkin, a sensible woman who believed in social occasions the way other people believed in God.

"Andrea, are you still there?" her mother said, impatient with Andie's long silence.

"Yes," Andie replied. "Thank you for calling, I've got to go now."

"One more thing, dear. Your father died of a heart attack at his home in San Diego last week."

The leaf twisted and broke off in Andie's hand. She was silent. Her fingers become numb around the receiver. She felt her body contracting, closing in on itself. San Diego! So close.

"Are you all right, dear?"

"Yes," Andie said, hating her mother for purposely dropping the news so casually.

"I'm sorry to upset you, but you haven't seen him since you were five years old. I doubt you even remember him."

"Of course I remember him," Andie said.

"Well, don't be too upset, dear. It's not like you really knew him."

Andie was silent.

"I'll tell you what, dear. I've got an event in Palm Springs next week. I'll just drive to Los Angeles and visit you. Won't that be nice?"

"Sure," Andie said without emotion.

"See you soon, Andrea."

Andie hung up the phone. She saw his face, the red beard that tickled when he kissed her, his cheeks flushed with laughter. Why had he left when she was five years old? Why had he never returned even for a visit? Her questions had never been answered before and now they never would be.

Sometimes in the middle of the night he had crawled into her small bed and hugged her tightly. For a while his arms had felt wonderful around her, but then she remembered being afraid and not knowing why.

* * * * *

"Andie, come down to the party," he had asked her the night of her mother's Spring Festival fund raiser. "How can I have any fun without my little lady running around. I want to hear you chatting with all your mother's fancy-dressed guests."

She had gone down to the party and she did just what he had asked. He gave her a few sips of wine until she felt light-headed and ran about talking with everyone.

"Do you like my dress? Daddy picked it out for me. I want a cracker with the pink stuff on top. It looks like tooth cream."

Normally she was shy around adults, but her father was the magic that made her bloom. He teased her sweetly until she laughed and talked with ease.

After the party her mother came quietly into her room, sat straight-backed at the edge of the child's bed, and told her she had something extremely important to say.

"Now, Andrea dear, I have a secret to share with you. This is a very special secret that only adults know. But after seeing you wildly running around with your father, flirting with everyone tonight, I thought you better know before it is too late."

Her voice was soft yet so frightening.

"Now listen carefully, dear. God gives every person on this earth just so many words, and when you use up all of your words you can't speak at all anymore. At the rate you were going tonight, you'll use up all your words before you get to be ten years old. Then you will have to be silent for the rest of your life."

The secret came as a complete surprise to Andie. She never thought it possible that people could run out of words. It seemed such an unfair thing to hear tonight just when she had begun to enjoy talking. Her skin turned icy cold. She wanted her mother's arms around her freezing body.

"Well, I just thought you should know. Your father is so careless, I didn't think he would ever tell you. Goodnight dear, sleep well," her mother said. She gave Andie a quick kiss on the forehead and left the room.

Andie lay awake for hours in silence. The party had been so exciting. With Daddy by her side, she'd felt grown-up...free. He made chatting so easy and fun. Now this secret changed everything. It was a terrifying new rule. She wanted to wake her father so that he could help her understand, but that would start a fight between her parents. Almost everything made them fight lately.

The next morning she raced from room to room in a panic looking for her father. The study was empty, so was the kitchen, the living room and her parent's bedroom. Gone. He was gone. But it was Sunday morning. Daddy always took her to the park on Sundays. Gone. She found her mother in the bathroom sitting on the side of the tub crying. She had never seen her mother cry before. It filled her with anger.

"Where's Daddy?" she demanded.

"Gone," her mother said. "Just gone."

"Why?" she cried.

After that day whenever Andie felt words begin to bubble up, threatening to explode into sound, she pretended that she had no mouth, no opening where words could escape. The pretend game grew. No eyes. With no eyes there were no tears. No ears or nose either. A week after the party Andie lay on the small patch of grass behind their Manhattan home all afternoon pretending to breathe the sun into her body through her skin. She watched the leaves of the fichus tree blowing in the breeze, feeding on the light.

Later that day her mother screamed at her. "How could you do this to yourself? Look at you! You are covered in heat rash."

Bumps covered her tiny body that was so sensitive to the bright light. A red-haired child with green eyes and white skin, she was easily set on fire by the sun. But Andie liked the strange sensation of heat all over her legs, arms, stomach and chest. It made her feel loved by the sun.

In December Andie had her sixth birthday and slowly stopped believing that her words would run out. But she had grown used to the quiet within herself. The joy of words had left with her father. She hardly ever spoke, especially to her mother.

Her childhood closet had been filled with fancy party dresses. A series of nannies had pulled them over her head and planted bows in her hair for her mother's parties. Now, without her father to tease her and make her laugh, she was shy. She dreaded her mother's public fawning sessions where she was forced to perform a silly song or poem to show everyone how clever she was. But the minute her moment was over, she was returned to her room.

Talking to the guests was not allowed. She felt like a polite addition to her mother's parties...a nice touch like a vase of spring daisies.

* * * * *

Andie sat at her desk at Metro Life after her mother's call. It was 5 p.m. Time to get back on the freeway...to go home to her canyon. She gathered up her philodendron and her Creeping Charlie and left her cubby hole.

Once on the freeway the traffic moved in slow motion. Andie began to panic. She was all alone, surrounded by crowds of people each in their own car prison. She sat in the endless jungle of cars longing to escape.

Her father was gone from her. She had missed him so much over all these years. Had he missed her?

When she told her mother she wanted to move to Los Angeles, she had expected an argument. Her mother would say that she was too young, too inexperienced to go so far away on her own. Andie knew all these things were true. How could she take care of herself? Live on her own in a city where she had no friends? But the protests from her mother never came. It had been the height of the social season and Mrs. Erkin had so many chairwoman responsibilities that she hadn't the time to take Andie's intentions seriously. Andie was terrified when she realized that no one would stop her; she was free to go.

The day before her move, the house had been filled with the frantic chaos of caterers and decorators before another one of her mother's gala fund-raisers.

"Andrea," her mother had said. "Will you please get out there and talk to people. You're a lovely girl. It's always such an embarrassment to parade such a silent daughter."

Andie bitterly remembered that as a child her words were the embarrassment. Now the embarrassment was her silence. Just as the guests began to arrive, Andie reminded her mother that she was going to Los Angeles in the morning.

"A little trip will do you good," her mother commented, as if she had forgotten that Andie intended much more than a trip. And with these words Andie was dismissed.

* * * * *

Andie didn't return to Metro Life the next day or ever.

A week later on Sunday afternoon, there was a knock at her door.

"Andrea, are you in there? It's your mother." The cottage was quiet. Then a low voice whispered, "Mother, is that you?"

Andie opened the door. Her mother gasped. "Good God! What's happened to you!"

"I'm fine, Mother, come in....it's messy but...."

"Andie, look at you. You look terrible! This is where you live? The path to this place is so badly overgrown I could hardly find the door. This is a falling-down shack in the middle of nowhere. You really must move."

She took her daughter's arms firmly in her hands. The skin felt slippery and transparent. "Are you sick? You look positively green."

"Mother, what are you doing here?"

"Don't sound so surprised. I told you I was coming in from Palm Springs. You sounded so upset about your father, I thought I better come."

"Why didn't he ever come back to see me," Andie asked.

"Well, you can thank me for that. I told the bastard if he ever tried to see you again, I'd tell the court about all the nasty things he did to you."

Andie's mind whirled. She remembered Daddy stealing into her room in the middle of the night—crawling into her bed—whispering to her. "I love you, Andie. No one will ever love you the way I do." Then his arms around her, his hands touching her.

"I'm here now," her mother said efficiently. "Everything is under control. I'll stay at the Hilton in Beverly Hills tonight and we'll fly back home to New York tomorrow. No arguments. It's clearly the best thing for you."

Andie drove her mother to the hotel that night. When she returned home she went directly into the garden. She began to see herself adapting to a new life—developing the retinas behind her green eyes until they no longer needed the light of day. She removed her shoes and socks then drooped her arms around the rose bushes, not feeling their thorns puncture her skin.

Her bare feet sank into the damp earth. She felt the nourishment course up through her toes like blood rushing into her veins. Bumps appeared on her arms and legs, burning at first, then breaking out into small brightly colored buds. Her finger tips spread into moist green leaves. Her breathing relaxed as the vines embraced her.

Uncommon Bonds

A unt Sadie and Aunt Nellie were born identical Siamese twins. Sadie's head pushed out first, but the joy of her birth lasted only a moment. To the horror of Dr. Bonner, who had delivered babies for almost half a century, beneath the head, coiled around the fragile neck, were two tiny feet. Nellie's entrance into the world provoked terrified screams from usually calm and proper nurses.

Sliding out together, Sadie and Nellie laid head to toe, joined at the middle. The immediate operation that separated their five pound bodies was much easier than anyone had expected when they first viewed the tangled, welded flesh. They shared no organs and only one major artery. The severing was a success. Both infants thrived physically.

The dramatic birth was headline news featuring before and after pictures of the tiny babies. Rose Hill wasn't just a dot on the state map. It had a respectable population of 25,000, but none of that number had been born connected to a sibling in anyone's memory. In the beauty shops and grocery stores people talked of almost nothing else for weeks.

The twin's parents, William and Sara Morgan, had always lived quietly with their only daughter, Ruth. William prided himself on being a private man. Even his growing reputation as a major American artist did not penetrate the walls of his studio. His indifference to New York's admiration only made him more intriguing and popular.

William Morgan was my grandfather, Ruth my mother. She was eight years old when the twins were born and everything changed forever in her life. Her father turned even more inward. He spent long hours etching the branch of a willow until it hung perfectly over a still summer pond. Sadie and Nellie's birth was beyond his artistic vision. Shortly after they were born, he left for Paris. My mother never saw him again. To his credit, he did send what money he could and many gifts over the next thirty years.

Aunt Sadie and Aunt Nellie were teenagers when I was born. They often baby sat for me, which they always did together. I remember being strangely afraid of these mirror image wonders in our family. When they walked into the house, I would run up to my room and worry if somewhere in the world there could be another girl child that looked exactly like me. Our home changed into a carnival with their presence.

Since they always dressed identically, I had trouble telling them apart. At bedtime they would tuck me in, sit on opposite sides of the bed, and read me stories. First Nellie would carefully pick a book from the stack on the shelves. She followed the words with her finger so that I could look at each word as she read it. Then

Sadie would take her turn. She showed me the pictures instead of the words as she told me the story. When I was old enough to begin recognizing words, I realized that Sadie never really read to me like Nellie. Sadie changed things as she went along, making up new characters and stories and not reading the words at all. That's how I remember telling my aunts apart—by their bedtime stories.

Over the years bizarre tales were told in the gossip underground of our small town about my two aunts. Sometime in their late twenties they rented an apartment together. It was rumored that they slept in the same bed, always with some part of their bodies touching, as if in sleep they sought to join their flesh again as it had been in the womb.

I remember only one family dinner when an outsider was invited to our home. It was Thanksgiving. I was fourteen and just beginning to discover that boys could be exciting. Aunt Sadie brought a date to dinner. He was about the best looking man I had ever seen. Blonde hair fell down over his forehead and he kept his wide smile fresh all evening in spite of the things that Nellie said.

"Just exactly what do you do for a living, Jeff?" Nellie had a way of making you feel that whatever answer you came up with, it wasn't the right one.

"Why, hasn't Sadie told you? I thought you two shared all your secrets."

He was teasing Nellie a little, but you could tell she was mad. Jeff was a secret that Sadie hadn't shared much with Nellie.

Sadie popped in to keep things calm. "Don't you remember, Nellie? I told you that Jeff got the job as football coach at Jefferson High School. He just started this year."

After everyone left, I helped my mother clean up the dishes.

"Do you think Sadie's going to marry Jeff?" I asked hopefully.

"She sure does seem to like him. I've never seen her so chatty."

"Are you two gossiping in here?" My father walked into the kitchen and gave my mother a little hug. "Wonderful dinner, Ruth."

"Beth wants to know if we're going to have a wedding."

"Not if Nellie has anything to say about it," my father laughed.

The New Year came with Jeff and Sadie still together. One night Aunt Sadie and I went up to my room and drew pictures of the perfect wedding dress.

"Has he asked you to marry him yet?"

"Almost," she said. "I think he's just waiting for the right moment."

But in February Nellie got pneumonia and insisted that Sadie go with her to Florida for the worst of the winter. It took Nellie months to get well. A marriage proposal finally came in the mail, but Sadie didn't feel she could leave Nellie alone. Time passed. Jeff started seeing the dance teacher at Jefferson High.

When they returned from Florida, my aunts began to spend all their time together. Mother started calling them my "maiden aunts." They got jobs working side by side as tellers at the First National Bank on Franklin Street. Whispers implied that Sadie and Nellie had an unearthly bond. In spite of the rumors, I knew my aunts to be extraordinary in no significant way. Above all they were polite, practical and had few expectations. Their lives were measured by the completion of small tasks.

The wedding dress drawings Sadie and I had done years ago became the patterns of my own wedding dress. Aunt Sadie and Aunt Nellie sewed it for me. Piles of lace covered the skirt and train. As I walked down the aisle, I saw Sadie smiling at me with tears rolling down her face. It was meant to be her dress, not mine. My heart was suddenly as full of sadness for her as it was with my own joy.

In their sixty-second year an extraordinary thing happened that dramatically changed the lives of my aunts. The highlight of each week for my aunts had been their Saturday projects. All through the week they would chat about the selected Saturday project. Anticipation was the truth behind their sweet bank teller smiles. That week's project was the attic. Not a chore but a memory treasure hunt, they looked forward to it as child might a trip to the zoo.

I was rarely invited to the Saturday ritual and the few times the offer was extended, I had found easy excuses to avoid what I perceived to be a tediously spent day. But this project required some energy and even a bit of physical strength, so my presence was necessary.

For hours the three of us resurrected old photo albums and cheap china relics. My aunts giggled and hugged one another with each new discovery. They were having a grand day.

"Here," Aunt Sadie cried in delight, "these are the drawings Daddy sent us in the years after he left." She pulled out a dozen or so pen and inks, yellowing with age. At first glance they looked quite ordinary to me. But then there was one that grabbed my eye.

"Give me that one!" I shocked my aunts with my sudden interest. My face flushed as I examined the drawing. Two angular faces within one, a women looking forward and sideways at the same time. The lines were as clear as a signature. There was no doubt in my mind that my grandfather had sent my aunts an original Picasso drawing. For over sixty years it had been stashed in a trunk in a dime store collection of an attic.

My excitement about the discovery created only a brief tangent in their otherwise lovely day. After a few minutes of staring at the Picasso, they were back into their treasure hunt. For a moment I envied the insulation that held their lives so tightly in place.

Aunt Sadie and Aunt Nellie did finally let me take the drawing to be authenticated and appraised. None of us was prepared for the verdict—an early Picasso worth at least half a million dollars.

Sadie wanted it auctioned off immediately. Her mind burned with the adventures so much money could bring. Nellie grew silent and afraid. The pattern of her life, the comfort of her daily existence was threatened. Never had she raised her voice in anger at her sister in all these years. They had always seemed to be of one mind. Selling the Picasso was the first decision of any magnitude where they found themselves on opposite sides of the argument.

The issue was debated for days. What started as a polite exchange of weakly held opinions grew into a desperate fight for what they both had come to believe was nothing less than their whole lives. A frantic call brought me racing over to arbitrate on what would otherwise have been a usual project Saturday. It was ten in the morning when I arrived to find my aunts on the porch drinking sherry in an icy silence. The soft brown hair of their youth had gone white at exactly the same time. Age lines framed their eyes at precisely the same angles. They didn't dress alike anymore; to the great relief of the whole family, they had stopped that in their twenties. But still I always had difficulty in telling them apart. Not a skin flaw or an age spot deviated on their round white faces.

"Help us," Nellie requested simply without even first offering a greeting. "Sadie won't understand that the drawing was a gift, a special gift from Father. A gift like that is not to be sold but kept for future generations."

Since I had a definite bias in this great debate, Nellie had selected a poor arbitrator. "What future generations? If you mean me and my family, I promise you we can all live without the Picasso. Nellie, we don't want to inherit grandpa's gift, we want you to sell it and spend the money yourself. Do all the things you never had the means to do."

Nellie's increasingly pointed chin jutted out in disapproval. "I thought we were perfectly happy here and suddenly she tells me that life should be an adventure. What is she talking about?" Nellie looked at me as if I could explain this mystery to her.

"Of course, we have been happy." The love and compassion in Sadie's voice touched me to the point of tears. They had been everything to each other and now a few lines on a piece of canvas would tear apart a lifetime of acceptance and commitment.

"I never wanted anything more either," Sadie tried to explain what she herself didn't understand. "I couldn't imagine anything more because I hadn't dared to imagine. Now my imagination won't let me sleep. I see everything that I only thought I could know through books and photographs; the red tile roofs covering Florence, that big clock in London and the statue of Churchill he made them promise to build right outside Parliament so that he could always keep an eye on the place. I want to see it all."

As she spoke, I knew with certainty that all these adventures would be hers if only her life was her own to create. I also knew that no matter how convincing Sadie tried to be, Nellie would never leave the house they had shared for so many years. That was Nellie's ace in the hole. She didn't believe that Sadie would travel the world without her and in the end she would give in and allow the drawing to stay in the attic.

Nothing was decided that day but a week later, early on a Monday morning Sadie came to my home with the Picasso tucked under her arm. "I can't do it myself," she said. You have to do it for me." She handed me the drawing.

"Does Aunt Nellie know about this?" I asked.

"No," was all she said.

I sold the Picasso at auction two months later. Nellie was silent when I told her. She didn't so much as look down at the check I handed them. The next day Sadie and Nellie walked into the First National Bank on Franklin Street as serious customers. They opened separate accounts.

The winter came and went and no mention was made of the money. Then in early April, Sadie announced the plans she had not breathed a word of even to Nellie. On May 3rd, Sadie was flying to New York, and after a week at the Plaza Hotel, she was sailing to Europe for an extended stay. No return date was determined.

On her last day at First National, they threw a huge retirement party. She laughed and said she wasn't retiring, she was beginning. On Saturday I took her the forty miles to St. Louis so that she could shop in the big city. What a day we had. Her closet full of blue and grey wool dresses would have been shocked by colors so bright. Both of my aunts had kept their tiny bodies and good figures, but I was still surprised to see how young and lovely Sadie looked trying on a red wrinkle free pant suit perfect for traveling. A child's smile lit her face all day.

Only once during the day did Sadie interrupt her pleasure to share her guilt with me.

"People must wonder what I am doing after all these years. They must think me terribly selfish."

I put my arms around her narrow back, "It doesn't matter what they think."

"Nellie doesn't say anything anymore. But I know how I have disappointed her." Her eyes began to water, "I worry so about her."

She was silent for a moment. I saw the image of their birth, as my mother had described it to me, Nellie's feet around Sadie's neck.

"It's time," I said.

The new clothes were politely modeled for Nellie when we got home. I saw no envy in Nellie's eyes, just sadness and quiet resignation. When Sadie put on the purple evening dress, we all three sat down to have tea together.

* * * * *

Sadie never did officially return from Europe. She met a gentleman in London. After six months of giddy letters telling us all about him, they were married in a civil ceremony in Brighton where her new husband lived. They came to visit us six months later.

Nellie and I waited eagerly for our first look at Sadie's prize. When the doorbell rang, I raced to greet them. Sadie hugged me then introduced me to Peter.

"I feel I already know you from all of Sadie's stories," he said, shaking my hand enthusiastically. A smile broke through his great red beard—a bear of a man with an English accent. I could have fallen in love with him myself.

"Now, let me meet my bride's twin," Peter said, entering the living room where Nellie sat quietly waiting.

Sadie rushed past him. "Nellie!" she cried. "I missed you so much." They held one another while Peter looked on confused.

I suddenly saw my aunts through Peter's eyes. How different they looked. Sadie's hair, now chestnut brown, was no longer cropped close to her small face but gently reached to her shoulders. Her face was full of the future while Nellie's face was a memory of the past. Peter could probably see the resemblance, but if he didn't know better, he might assume them to be at least fifteen years apart. He paused a moment, then he bounced into the room.

"My God," he said kindly. "You are the mirror image of one another."

The Beam Walker

We are escaping. Making a run for it before Dad wakes up and finds us gone. Mom dragged me out of bed when it was still dark. She didn't even make me get dressed, just stuffed me in the car in my pajamas. We rolled silently out of the driveway and didn't start the engine until we hit Elm Street at the bottom of our hill. Once on the parkway, Mom really hit the gas.

I hope we pass a McDonald's soon. An Egg McMuffin is what I need. But it's only 4:30 a.m. and nothing is open yet.

"Go to sleep, Scott, honey. I'll wake you up when we find a place to eat." Mom's driving our old Ford like a bat out of hell.

After a few hours, it starts to get light out. We're going north, leaving Chicago and our Lincoln Park house far behind. No school for me today. The sixth grade won't be the same without me. Mrs. Castle will think I'm cutting again. One town after another flies by, Evanston where Grandma lives, then Highland Park, and finally across the Wisconsin border into Kenosha.

I crawl into the back seat, unzip the smashed suitcase, and pull out a T-shirt and pants. Can't find any underwear. It's 7:30 now, so we got to hit a McDonalds soon. Time to get dressed.

Tears are rolling down Mom's cheeks. " It's O.K.," I tell her. "We're gonna make it. This is the great escape." She smiles just a little and says, "Right, the great escape."

At last, a Burger King. I'm starving. The place is full of big guys with baseball caps, truck drivers, I guess. The food-ordering line takes forever. These guys are all getting a shit load of stuff.

"Mom, can I get a burger and fries even if it's supposed to be breakfast?"

"Whatever you want, Scott." She doesn't care. All she gets is coffee.

It seems so weird, just the two of us sitting alone at a table for four. For a second I think I see Ben in the empty chair across from me and I want to tease him about the geeky hat he always wears with the dumb monkey on it. Mom puts her arm around me. I think she can see Ben, too. If we see him hard enough together, maybe we can make him really be there. He would be eating his burger with so much ketchup it would be squirting out the sides all over his shirt, and if Dad were here, he would be yelling his lungs out at Ben for being such a slob. But if Dad were here, we wouldn't be running away.

Meals were always a fight at our house. I think Dad liked it that way, lots of action. If he wasn't complaining about the food, he was picking on me or Ben about anything he could think of. In between he told us stories about how brave he was. Some of them were exciting and we liked to listen, but mostly they were all the same. My Dad was a Beam Walker and all his stories were about how great he was.

"You kids pay attention now. When we were first building the Sears Tower, Bill and I were the only beam walkers in the Iron Workers Union. We walked the steel grids one hundred stories up and never blinked an eye." He had a million Sears Tower stories.

It was Dad's job, but it was also his obsession. That's what Mom called it, his obsession. It was a word I got to know real well. Two summers ago when Ben was seven and I was ten, Dad decided it was time we learned his trade. He took us up on the roof of our apartment building and told us to walk around the whole thing on the edge. I cried and begged him not to make me do it, but Ben followed Dad right out on the stone ledge. Dad danced along never looking down. Ben put one foot in front of the other, concentrating like when he was eating an ice cream sundae or something else he really liked. He was more afraid of Dad than he was of falling the four stories off the building.

"Come on, Scott, get out here. Are you gonna let your little brother show you up?"

It sounded like a friendly challenge, but I knew there was nothing friendly in it. If I didn't walk the ledge myself, he would make me.

The closer I got to the edge, the sicker I felt. My stomach was coming up through my throat. Just a few feet more, I thought, when I threw up all over myself. That just made Dad madder. He picked me up and jumped out onto the ledge. When I looked down, my legs were sticks hanging in mid-air as he held me over the side. When he put me down on the roof, I collapsed. My body was like a dead fish, no bone and no muscle. Well, at least it's over, I thought, and I'm still alive. But it wasn't over, not by a long shot. Dad kept my brother and me up there all afternoon walking the ledge. He coached us like we were learning to play baseball or something.

"Take a good look at this ledge, kids." He was standing at the very edge drinking a beer. "It's almost two feet wide. Just a narrow sidewalk. Anybody can walk on it real easy. The fear is all in your mind. Just remember to relax, keep your body straight, use your arms for balance, and don't look down."

All his teaching never made it any easier for me. I just learned to stop throwing up. Both Ben and I finally walked around the whole building on the ledge. Dad was cheering us on and promising us a banana split reward. Now we were his heroes.

"I'm so proud of you guys." Then he hugged us in his huge arms, I thought he would crush me. He was like a bear with thick black hair and this big head all scruffy and powerful looking.

The next year we moved into the house in Lincoln Park. Mom said she wanted a garden and her own home, but I know she just wanted to get us off the roof. But that didn't stop Dad. He would take us to construction sites and make us walk the beams. Ben hated it as much as I did, but the difference was he got good at it. He had Dad's natural balance. I just decided that it was okay if I died, then at least Dad would be sorry and never make Ben be a beam walker when he grew up.

Last month Dad took us to his job site on a Sunday when no one was working. We took the elevator up to the seventeenth floor. "This is the day of graduation," he said. "My sons graduate today." Ben's lips were purple. His skin turned white and bloodless. "No," he said. "I can't do it." It was the first time Ben stood up to Dad. I was so proud of him that for a moment I didn't realize how useless his words were.

"Just for that, you can go first, Ben." Then he softened his voice and pulled out all his encouraging words. "You can do it! I know you can. You're my son and you're not afraid of anything."

"But I am afraid, Dad. Please don't make me do it." Ben was shivering like it was the middle of winter and he had no clothes on. I wanted to grab Ben and run away forever, but there was no place to run.

As if he could read my mind, Dad said, "If you run away from the things you're scared of, you'll be running all your life. You've got to face your fears straight on. Can't you boys see I'm doing this for you? Once you walk this beam, you can do anything in life. You'll never be afraid of anything again."

Mom finished her third cup of coffee, and we left the Burger King. "How far north are we goin?" I asked.

"I don't know yet, honey. Once we get into Canada, I've got a cousin who is going to help us. I called her last night. She knows we're coming. There's an old summer cottage in the mountains her family has had for twenty years. We'll stay there until we decide where to go next." When she put her arms around me I felt like crying, so I closed my eyes and saw Ben sailing down through the air, and I just imagined that he could fly like an angel and never hit the ground.

Yesterday, Dad had knocked on my door and said we were going out. When Dad first came to take us to practice, Mom would try and stop him, but he ignored her. After a while, she just sat in the kitchen saying her rosary beads. This time was different. Mom put her five-foot-one body in front of his six foot bulk and screamed, "No, you can't have Scott." I remembered how much good it had done Ben to stand up to Dad. But he backed off. "O.K., maybe not today. But you got to get right back up on the horse. Grief is just another kind of fear and you can't let it own you."

Mom is driving slower now; not so crazy as when we left this morning. I decide to crawl into the back seat and sleep. The suitcase is open and stuff is falling out everywhere. My eye catches Ben's green, geeky, monkey hat. I curl up with the hat and wonder if it will be cold in Canada.

The Fuller Brush Man

I t is our ceremony. Every night just before bedtime, my mother brings me into her room and sits me down in the velvet-covered chair before the dressing table.

An oval mirror tray lies perfectly in the center. The gold coil rim around it creates a miniature fence safeguarding delicate perfume bottles. I love the perfumes because they are held in tiny crystal containers that reflect the lights and splash into a dozen colors in the mirror.

Beside the mirror are my mother's hair brushes with dark wood handles that always feel smooth and warm in my small hands. I choose one of many brushes and give it to my mother. She gently draws it through my hair one hundred times every night. Sometimes she sings to me as she brushes but mostly she just hums, a low sweet sound.

Mother buys her combs, brushes, and perfumes from the Fuller Brush man. He goes from door to door with his case of beautiful brushes. I know him. He has come to our house many times over the years. I call him Mr. Peabody. His name is Burt Orville, but he looks like a Peabody to me. His head is too small for his body and his glasses are too big for his head. His shirt fits so loose at the neck that I imagine he could stuff a whole other person in there. I guess he is shy because he never looks at me straight in the eye. When he visits, I peek around the entrance hall corner and listen to him talking with my mom.

"Got some new barrettes here I think you'll like. Made of real turtle shell. Do you want to have a look?" Mr. Peabody says.

"I don't think so. I've been wearing my hair short. I don't need any barrettes."

"Well, what about that pretty little daughter of yours? Her long blonde hair would fix up real nice in one of these turtle shell barrettes." I giggle when he says those things about me. She always ends up buying something from Mr. Peabody. He calls her his favorite, good, regular customer.

It is a hot August day. My mother is on her knees poking at the icebox. "Broken," she tells me. "It's so darn hot in this house everything is going to spoil in about ten minutes. I'll run to the store and get some ice. Come with me."

"Oh, Mom, I don't want to go. I'm playing with my dolls."

"I don't like you staying alone. You are only seven and that's not old enough to stay alone." But she gives in. "I'll just run to the store and be back in thirty minutes or so. You stay right here. Don't leave the house, not even to play in the backyard. Understand?"

Staying alone doesn't worry me. I'm not scared of anything.

A few minutes after she leaves, the doorbell rings. Through the screen door I see Mr. Peabody with his brush case. "Hi there, little honey," he says. "Mom isn't home." I tell him. "Well, I'll just come in and leave these little samples," he says. For a few seconds I don't know what to do because my mother told me never to let anyone in the house when she isn't home. But I think she said strangers and Mr. Peabody isn't a stranger; he's the Fuller Brush man. I unlock the screen door.

He walks in the house and puts the samples on the side board. Then he turns around and looks at me straight in the eye. I feel weird—he is looking at me so strange. "You look real pretty today all dressed up in that cotton jumper."

"I'm not dressed up." I say defiantly.

Then he walks right into the living room and sits in the easy chair. "Come here," he says. I don't move.

"Come here," he says again. "What are you afraid of? I don't bite."

"I'm not afraid." And just to prove it, I walk right up to him.

He grabs my waist and pulls me down on his lap. "Stop!" I scream.

"Be quiet or you might get hurt." He twists my arm behind my back. I stop screaming. My voice disappears. I'm afraid to move.

"I just want to see how pretty you really are." He puts his hand down on my chest and rubs me. I feel sick. He moans and sticks his hand up my skirt. He puts his fingers between my legs and rubs real hard. His moaning gets louder. I feel I might throw up. He moans so loud, I think he is going to die.

Then suddenly he stops, lets me go, and runs out of the house. I am afraid to move. When my legs feel alive again I crawl to my parent's room and hide under the bed.

* * * * *

I don't know what happened to Mr. Peabody. He never came to our house again.

I wouldn't sit at my mother's dressing table anymore. The brushes looked like small dead animals. I was terrified of them.

Then one day the brushes were gone. "I put them away," my mother told me. After that we spent many nights at her dressing table putting on make-up and singing. But she never brushed my hair again.

Gray Lake

rad tossed his suitcase in the back of the VW van. "Come on Jasper," he called. "We're pushing off." A long-haired black mutt came racing out from the back yard and leapt into the van. "Don't look so excited," Brad said. "This is not a pleasure trip."

Going back to Denton hadn't really been a decision, just something Brad knew it was time to do. Maybe hitting forty was part of it. He had celebrated the birthday by walking on the beach alone with Jasper. Kids surfed in the late afternoon waves, screaming excitedly at one another. Brad watched them, envying their easy friendships and relaxed fun. Sometimes there had been a girlfriend, but nothing lasted. He ached to be out in the water, a kid again. He tossed a stick into the ocean and Jasper tore after it.

When Brad had left Denton, Texas, he was twenty years old and the town hero. It was the year after the Summer Olympics of 1968. He was in only one event, platform diving. The town went wild when he returned that summer with his long, thin body and his gold medal. The victory parade was aired on national hook-ups making him an instant legend.

He remembered the exhilaration when the gold medal was placed around his neck and The Star Spangled Banner filled his head. The moment stopped time, allowing him to believe that nothing would be beyond his grasp ever again. Then he had gone home to the hero's parade to see Mary Alice waving along with all the other admirers. But before the joyous smile that he had saved especially for her could form itself, he saw her left hand firmly held by Billy Carlson. Brad managed a forced grin for the rest of the parade so that the town could have its hero.

Being worshiped because he could plummet gracefully ten meters through the air had gotten old fast for Brad. He was the gold medal winner in Denton, but that's all he would ever be. Whatever else he did in his life, people would still talk about his finest hour. So he headed west to Los Angeles, leaving his glory behind.

Living alone got Brad into the habit of talking to his dog. At first it seemed normal enough, but then he began to believe that Jasper understood everything he said. On Sundays they would go for long hikes in the Santa Monica Mountains where Brad talked to the dog about everything. "So what do you think, Jasper? Should I quit this damn job? Sitting in front of a computer all day can get to be pretty lonely."

"You think I'm crazy going back to Denton, don't you?" Brad said to the dog as they hit the San Diego Freeway. Jasper curled up in the back seat making no comment. "Good idea, boy. Go to sleep. Texas is a long drive and we aren't in any hurry to get there."

Late on the second day they crossed from Arizona into New Mexico. The scenery turned to desert boredom. Brad passed the time by conjuring up Mary Alice's picture in the senior year book that he had kept in his bedroom for the last twenty years, her face frozen, perpetual glowing youth. They pulled over for a walk. Jasper was delighted for the chance to run until he saw a rattlesnake stretched out basking in the sun. The dog made a hasty retreat back to the safety of the van. The temperature outside was closing in on one hundred and six and the 1982 van's air conditioner was reaching its limit. "I know what you're thinking," Brad looked back at the hanging face of his old dog. "We should have waited to make this trip in the winter instead of mid-August." Jasper whined in agreement.

Noon on the third day they hit Texas. As they got closer to Denton, the memories began to come back. Diving into cool water. Flying through the air in perfect control. Brad could almost feel his bare feet on the metal steps as he climbed up to the platform, stretching his strong calves with each lift. Then standing at the edge, so far above the water, preparing himself mentally for the dive.

A truck flashed its signal, pulled out and blared past him. "Got to keep my mind on driving, not daydreaming. Wake up, Jasper! Come up here and keep me company." The dog climbed down from the back seat, had a drink of water from the dish on the floor, then jumped up into the passenger's seat. "That's better. Can't have much of a conversation with you sitting all the way in the back."

"Denton, 20 miles. See that, Jasper? This is it. Our last chance."

A sign flashed $36 a night—color TV. Brad pulled over and parked the van. "None of these old broken down places will take a dog, Jasper. You'll have to lay low until we get the room key, then I can smuggle you in." Brad walked over to the office.

The motel owner looked about ninety with hearing to match, so at least the dog wasn't going to be a problem. "How long you want the room for?" the old guy asked.

The question caught Brad off guard; he hadn't quite thought that one out yet. "Not sure," he said finally. "Put me down for three days and I'll let you know. Can you give me a room at the back—away from the noise of the traffic?"

Brad moved the van directly in front of unit twenty-nine. He quickly hustled Jasper into the motel room where the dog lost no time in making himself comfortable on the saggy double bed. Even though the dog fell asleep, Brad talked to him for hours about his plans for his first day in Denton in twenty years.

* * * * *

The VW van pulled up to the town's only high school at 10:00 a.m. It was still a few weeks before the kids came back, so everything was quiet. Brad and Jasper walked around behind the gym to the Olympic sized pool Brad had made famous. It looked the same, as if time had stopped for all those years. There was a padlock on the gate. "Jasper, you stay here. Keep a lookout for me." Brad climbed over the ten foot metal fence and dropped down near the diving boards. For a long time he sat on the low springboard and stared at the blue water. Then he stripped off his clothes leaving himself covered in only his red Olympic competition diving suit that still fit his trim body. Jasper stuck his nose through the fence whining.

Brad walked to the ladder of the platform board. He climbed slowly just as he had in his daydream the afternoon before. Standing at the top, he looked down and in his mind the empty bleachers filled with people shouting, "Go for it, Brad. You can do it!" Then his eye caught one special face in the crowd, Mary Alice Heller. She smiled up at him with an angel's face. He walked out to the edge of the platform silently dedicating his dive to her.

This was his first look at the water from ten meters up in twenty-one years. The gold medal dive had been his last. He wondered if his body would remember. He visualized himself executing all the different dives he had mastered. He wanted to pick the right one—the one that would bring him the highest score—so many things to think about: the degree of difficulty, the danger, the dive that would best show off his flexibility, balance, strength and grace. His front three and a half in pike position had been a dazzler. But then those twisters with their demand for precise timing always brought him high marks.

Brad stood with only his toes touching the edge of the platform. He practiced each dive in his mind. He heard Mary Alice say, "please, just tonight, can't you forget diving practice for one night?" No, he never could. Not even the night of the senior prom. It was too close to the Olympic trials and every hour counted.

Staring down at the water, Brad counted. How many hours, days, years had he given to this hard platform? He had started diving at eight years old. That made eleven years until his final gold medal dive. Eleven years of climbing a metal ladder alone. Eleven years of practicing to do one thing brilliantly. Years when he saw his friends go to movies and dances without him. All he had to display for those eleven years was a gold medal on a faded ribbon.

Brad bent his knees, pushed off from the balls of his feet and dove straight into the pool. No somersaults or twists, he went into the water perfectly perpendicular, without a splash.

Jasper began barking when Brad dropped from the platform and didn't stop until Brad emerged from the water.

* * * * *

Once Jasper was carefully smuggled back into the "no pets" motel, Brad went to the office to borrow a telephone book. There was no Mary Alice Heller listed. He walked back to the room.

"She probably doesn't live here anymore," he told Jasper. "And even if she does, she's listed under a husband's name. Maybe we should go to Gray Lake together, Jasper. Forget about Mary Alice." Jasper jumped down from the bed and started scratching a hole in the corner of the carpet. "O.K.," Brad gave in. "I'll try one more thing, but that's all."

The next morning Brad went to the new Denton Public Library. He asked to look at the microfilm of The Denton Evening Post. After only two hours he found what he was looking for. "Mr. and Mrs. Thomas Heller are happy to announce the marriage of their daughter, Mary Alice, to Darryl Baker."

The librarian directed Brad to a public telephone behind the fiction shelves. Mary Alice Baker. She was listed in the Denton telephone directory. Slowly he dialed the number waiting to hear that voice from his past.

"Hello," a woman answered.

For a moment Brad was speechless. It was the same voice he had heard so often in his dreams. "Mary Alice?" Her name was all he could get out.

"Who is this?" she asked sounding frightened.

"I hope you still remember me. It's Brad—Brad Stockert."

"I don't believe it," she cried. "Where are you calling from?

You're not here in Denton, are you?"

"Yes, but only for a few days. It would be great to see you again."

When Brad got back to the van, he grabbed Jasper and hugged him. "She's going to see us this afternoon. She's got three kids, all teenagers. Christ, I can't believe it. All I got is you, Jasper. No offense.

"We've got three hours to kill before we see Mary Alice. What should we do, Jasper? How about I show you where I grew up?" Brad drove to the house on Brooks Street where he had lived most of his early years. The old Tudor still looked impressive. Eleven rooms, including five bedrooms, three of which were empty most of the time since Brad was an only child. There was a huge attic upstairs where Brad had played for hours by himself. Three years after he had left for California, his parents sold the house to take a small apartment. The place is just too big, his father had said. The truth was it was always too big; so much space with only three people to fill it. Brad looked at his watch. "It's time, Jasper. We're off to see Mrs. Baker."

* * * * *

The visit with Mary Alice felt awkward and formal. She introduced him to her kids. He introduced her to Jasper. They all worked hard at sounding relaxed. How could twenty years have passed, Brad thought, as he watched her getting them all sodas and snacks. Everything about her was the same yet everything was different. Her body was no longer slim. She had cut her glorious long blonde hair almost as short as his own. But she still put her hands in front of her mouth when she laughed as if the steel braces remained forever visible across her now perfect teeth. And the voice was the same as the young girl he remembered, its unique timbre still touched his heart.

On the mantel a wedding photo took the center spot with snapshots of the kids at various ages all around it. Brad tasted envy as the frozen images of the smiling family stared at him. He needed to get out of the house.

"Look," he said. "It's a beautiful day. Why don't we take a little ride? I'd like to see Gray Lake again."

Mary Alice hesitated. "What about you, kids? Want to go out to the lake?" They had no interest in a ten mile drive to spend the afternoon with Mom and some old friend. So it was just the three of them: Brad, Mary Alice and Jasper.

"Do you remember when we used to come out to Gray Lake?" Brad said. "We'd get a boat, row out to the middle and just lay there kissing under the stars."

"They still rent boats here," she teased him. "Can Jasper swim?"

The three of them got a fishing boat with an outboard. The lake reflected the whole sky in the late afternoon sun. "I never knew why they named this Gray Lake," Brad said. "It's crystal clear."

"It didn't have anything to do with the color," Mary Alice laughed. "William Steven Gray owned most of this county even before Denton became a town. The lake's named after him."

"Well, I'll be damned. I lived here nineteen years and I never knew that. Things are never what they seem."

"Why are you here, Brad?" she asked, suddenly serious. "This isn't just a casual drop by."

"When we were dating in high school, I always thought that you and I would end up together." Brad petted the dog to avoid Mary Alice's eyes. "I was so crazy in love with you."

"You made your choice a long time ago, remember. You picked the Olympics, not me. I felt so guilty every time there was a diving meet. I'd pray for you to lose."

"I wish I had lost. Maybe I really did lose. Eleven years of diving doesn't teach you much about living or talking to people. Look," he laughed, "this is my best friend." Brad scratched Jasper behind the ears. "You went to the prom with Billy Carlson. When I got back from the Olympics, you were practically going steady with him. So I decided to leave Denton."

"You never called me after you came back."

"I thought it was over; that you didn't care anymore. I was afraid to call." They turned off the motor, letting the boat drift.

"You want to know why I came here now? For this," Brad said, pulling a small velvet packet from his pants pocket. He handed it to Mary Alice. "Open it."

Inside the velvet lay the Olympic gold medal with the ribbon still attached. "What does this mean?" she asked.

"If it weren't for that thing my whole life would have been different. We might be out on this lake celebrating our anniversary, or I don't know, I might have my own kids.

"Thanks for coming here with me, Mary Alice. Jasper and I didn't want to have to do this alone." Brad gently took the gold medal from her hand. "I came here to say goodbye to my mistakes so that I could move on." Brad held the medal over the side of the boat. Its gold reflection bounced on the surface of the water. He let the ribbon slip from between his fingers, watching as the gold medal sank into the clear lake.

The Black Swan

The huge fireplace with its mighty earth stones covers a full wall of the tavern. I wonder when the bloody thing was built. It must be at least two or three hundred years old...probably part of some grand lord's castle back in the 13th century. Well, it's my home now...this tavern.

There's a tavern for every day's ride in the countryside of England these days. But none of them compare to the jewels we got here in the Cotswolds. This is the best bloody land in the country. The soil's so rich you can eat it. Deep red it is, full of iron and steel. The kids grow strong here and their faces is rosy red as the soil. I know. I lived here all my life. Born just two miles west of the Black Swan, I was. Always knew I would end up working in the Swan one day.

Not that I'm complaining. It's a good life, it is. The men that come in here, they like a strong red-faced wench like me. First thing they see when they come through that heavy wooden door is me...long black hair with eyes to match. They smile at me right off and I know they're thinking, "Well, there's the Black Swan herself."

Now don't start supposin' that I am all full of myself. There is plenty a girls around that are prettier than me. I don't mean to be bragging. It's just that I know I fit here and the men, they know it too. See, the locals go to the Bull and the Rose, that's their tavern. The men that come into the Black Swan are gentlemen. Mostly tired and thirsty from the three-day ride from London. They come to trade goods, to buy market wares that can only be found in the Cotswolds, or I fancy, they come to see me.

I do lots more than serve the beer and the men, if you know what I mean. When they get to drinkin', making-up wild songs, tellin' jokes, and playing their wits against each other, I ain't shy to say I can keep up with the best of them. Many a night we laugh and sing until dawn. It's best when Bobby's the one that keeps me laughing. A real teaser that one is. Pinches my bottom rough, makes fun of me with his bawdy jokes. But when he's got me in his arms he's as gentle as a lamb, and his touch is soft cool lace. He's twenty-three, same as me, but with all his worldly ways I feel like a child with him. His hair is sandy blond and it always hangs like a weeping willow cross his forehead.

"Come on, girl," he calls. "Are you going to just sit there when my legs are aching for a dance?" He swings me up into his arms and we circle the floor as the fiddler saws the Jolly Robin. Sometimes when we're dancin' he gets a bit sloppy with his steps, and when I'm off balance he lets his hands fly all over my body before I find my feet. He's always the last to leave.

In bed, after, he looks real serious. Then straight into my heart he talks to me like I'm his best friend. "My Father says it's time I stopped spending so much time riding the road. He wants me to learn the business in London and stay put. Can you imagine me in a yardage store all day managing a business?"

"I can't imagine you anywhere but here," I say, and that's the truth. I've never been to London, let alone a proper yardage store.

"It's with you that I want to be," Bobby says, and I believe him. I know he laughs and plays more with me than he ever will with the ladies of London. But I'm not for marrying and they are. Oh, I see the fine ladies that come to the famous Cotswold market, carried in their gilded coaches drawn by white, perfectly groomed horses. The other girls at the Black Swan glow green with envy and wish they'd been born to a higher state. But I think only of Dill, my sweet grey mare. With her between my legs we gallop the hills and the moors. What do I want with carriages and gold? The wild marigolds are my gold. The wind and speed are my carriage.

These fine ladies are lifeless white-faced dolls to me. Their perfect posture held in place with sharp stays digging into their ribs. I've seen them eat, so dainty with the right fork. Give me the Black Swan with its huge stone hearth and they can take their fancy parlors and perfect manners. I swing my bare leg across a bar stool. "One day Bobby, my sweet love, you'll stop comin'. You'll leave me for a fine lady of your own class."

"Never," he swears. But we both know the day is soon. I'll never find the likes of him again in my life and knowin' that puts a sad pain in my heart.

I walk the heath just before the dawn breaks. I take off my shoes and feel the red earth slide between my toes. The ground is scattered with smooth worn stones. Three hundred years ago someone gathered stones like these and built the Black Swan's mighty hearth. This is my home.

The first rays of the sun lick the sky behind the hills. I run back to the tavern barn to harness Dill. This is the perfect hour to mount my mare and ride.

Claire's Oath

There is a gentle touch on the small of my back. Then more of a shove along my right leg. Sleep holds me tightly until my shoulders begin to shake and a voice utters my name. "Claire, honey, wake-up." The sound breaks through my alpha waves.

"It's Lydia," my husband, Mark, says.

"What's Lydia," I reply, looking at his half open brown eyes pleading with me for understanding.

"The phone. It's Lydia on the phone."

"What time is it?" I ask.

This strikes him as funny. A tiny grin turns up the left corner of his mouth.

"Guess," he says.

"Guess! What do you mean guess?" I ask, unable to follow this bend in the conversation.

"Guess what time it is."

"What do you mean, guess." I am now fully awake. "It is the

middle of the damn night. I'm not guessing. Give me the phone."

He puts the cordless in my hand and turns over, stuffing his head contently back into the pillows.

"Did I wake you?" Lydia's voice booms through the receiver.

"Of course you woke me." I glance at the glowing red light on the clock radio and discover that it is 2 a.m. "Call me tomorrow."

"Don't hang up. I need your help. It will only take a minute."

Lydia always needs my help and it never takes a minute. We have been friends for over thirty years. I've known her longer than my husband or my children.

"Let me take it downstairs," I say knowing that hanging up on Lydia is useless. She will only call back and wake Mark again. He is now peacefully snoring. It is no wonder he can find his sense of humor in the middle of the night...he knows he can be back asleep in seconds. Once I'm awake, that's it for the rest of the night. I click off the cordless, pull on my robe and climb down the stairs to the living room.

"So, what's the drama this time?" I ask, settling into the barcalounger with the phone that has the soft headrest glued to it. I might be here a while if this is another one of Lydia's confusing stories.

"I'm at Ian's apartment."

"At two in the morning! Where does Doug think you are?"

"With you."

I had been her cover through three affairs and each time things got more risky.

"Lydia, what are you doing with me in the middle of the night?"

"Let's think of something fast because Doug might call you

any second."

"Why are you still with Ian?"

"I'll fill you in later. Right now we need to get some facts together. I just called Doug and told him we were watching a movie and we fell asleep. I said I was coming home right away."

"Fine. So why are you waking me up?"

"Because I don't think he bought it. He's got a suspicious mind."

"I wonder why?"

"So if he calls, I trust you can handle it."

"Clearly trust is not an issue here. Goodnight, Lydia."

I go to the kitchen and pop a cup of milk into the microwave. It never does put me back to sleep but I can't drop the hope that it will. I watch the seconds tick off on the microwave, amazed that two minutes takes so long. How can a whole day go by like a lightning flash when it is composed of thousands of these tiny two minute bites? Three, two, one...then three short bings. I take the warm milk into the living room and wait for Doug's call. This lie should be easy. I'll be back to bed not sleeping in no time.

Lydia and I had become best friends in middle school. We didn't make the cheerleading squad and took comfort in getting drunk together at Lord's Park. When our tears of rejection and a bottle of screw-top Gallo wine had dried up, we showed off our loudest cheers to the overfed ducks.

Lydia had danced about kicking her long legs into the air and jiggling her new breasts. How I had wanted her body instead of mine. She had become a woman that year and took joy in displaying her curves to all the eager boys. When they saw her coming down the hall at school, their eyes narrowed like those of little white rats hungry and nervous. They watched her bend over in her tight short skirt as she gathered her gym clothes from the floor of her locker. I could see them aching to clutch the cheeks of her perfect young ass. They never noticed me. I was still a girl, skinny, flat-chested, and short.

Stumbling around on the grass that night, we had started to giggle about the Vanderford twins with identical fat bottoms who had made the cheerleading squad. Their little cherub faces would delight the fans until they turned around and with their fannies in the air, cheered "push 'em back, push 'em back, waaay back." We laughed so hard we both coughed up red wine all over our new school jackets.

Forgetting the cold of that October night, we stripped naked and jumped into the freezing pond. Shivering, we stood in the shallow water, put our palms together and raised our hands up to the full moon. We swore that night at Lord's Park to be best friends for life, to tell each other all our secrets and to always be loyal to each other. It had been a drunk but solemn ritual.

So here I was at two in the morning, a forty-six year old woman with two grown children, still keeping that ridiculous oath.

I'm sitting in the living room waiting for Doug's call for almost a half hour now. Just as I decide to go back to bed the phone rings. I take a deep breath. Lying always makes me tense.

"Hello," I say much too brightly for the middle of the night.

"Claire, this is Doug. Is Lydia there?"

"No. She just left. Maybe ten minutes ago. She should be home soon."

"What movie were you watching?"

Oh, God. Now what am I suppose to say? I start improvising. "It was an old British film, slow and boring. We both fell asleep."

"What was the name of the movie, Claire?"

I feel like I'm on the witness stand as he grills me with questions. Where did we go for dinner? What did Lydia order? I make up answers chatting away as if nothing is wrong. His accusing tone softens. He apologizes for calling me so late. Worry creeps into his voice. I tell him she'll be home soon. We hang up.

I call Lydia's cell to update her on what she needs to know. A man's voice answers. It's Ian. He tells me that Lydia ran out five minutes ago and left her cell at his place. How the hell can she have forgotten her phone! She just called me. My hands get clammy as panic sets in. Doug will confront Lydia with all the same questions when she gets home and she won't have a clue what the answers are. Somehow I've got to talk to her before she talks to Doug. I race upstairs to get dressed. The only way is to drive to Lydia's house and catch her before she goes in. I hate this overwhelming feeling of loyalty that forces me to act irrationally.

Mark wakes up as I jump into dirty sweats.

"Honey, what's going on?"

"I'll explain in the morning. Go back to sleep."

"You're going out at this hour?" He is angry and disappointed in me. "Why can't you just once let her pay the price for screwing up?"

"I'm sorry, but I have to go. It's our deal. She needs me."

"But you don't need her."

I rush out to the car. The streets are empty. If I drive sixty, I might be able to beat her home. Why do I feel this crazed need to protect Lydia? Her marriage isn't worth risking my life for. I remember when she decided to marry Doug ten years ago. It was the only thing she ever did for logical reasons. The rest of her life followed her impulses but Doug was a solid practical decision, a move towards stability, a statement to the world that she was to be taken seriously. He was a publisher complete with reputation and family money. The night before the wedding I asked the previously unspoken question. "Do you love him?" She flippantly replied, "Of course, I love everything that he is."

When I arrive at Lydia and Doug's home, I half expect to see her red Mercedes already sitting in the circular driveway. My heart is pounding like it did in the middle of our last 6.1 earthquake. At least that was a real event manufactured by nature and not by Lydia. Her car is not here. I beat her home. Slowly I drive past the three story Tudor house and park down the block. I figure the minute she drives up, I'll give a quick honk, get her attention, feed her all the answers to Doug's question, and get back home.

It feels eerie sitting alone in my car at night. I remember the last time Lydia needed my help was three months ago. She had been arrested by the Coast Guard for breaking into a yacht in Marina del Rey. They found her naked with a twenty-two year old bartender she had picked up at The Gray Pelican a few hours earlier. Lydia usually took the complications she brought into her life in stride, but that time she was a bit too close to actually going to jail. It might be hard to hide things like bail and a court appearance from Doug. I had gone down to the harbor at four in the morning to rescue her. The Coast Guard guys were not city police. They had a different view of the law and, fortunately, a sense of humor. They were looking for drugs, not sex, when they found Lydia. I sweet-talked them into forgetting the whole incident by explaining that Lydia and her bartender did not actually break in. They simply unsnapped the blue canvas and discovered the hatch was unlocked.

Lydia was grateful. She took me to dinner at the Polo Lounge the next night. I got the whole story of what happened on the boat.

"His name was Adonis," she told me. "Can you believe a mother naming her kid Adonis! Each time he brought me a drink, he would gently touch my hands. After the third drink, he put his index finger into my Marguerite and touched the wet finger to my lips. He was so hot."

Lydia's life was clearly more colorful than mine. I felt old, married, jealous, and wonderfully excited listening to her. I noticed several men in the restaurant staring at Lydia with that same hungry look that school boys had once displayed. She was still a knockout in her perfectly tailored backless evening dress. As she told me all the details of The Adonis Affair, I looked at her thin face and body. The full breasts of our Lord's Park days had vanished with rigorous diets and millions of hours of exercise. Tall and toned at forty-six, she had the look of a Paris model. Lydia and I had reversed our body types over the years. She had aged into the skinny, flat-chested girl I had been and I had a middle-aged roundness, complete with heavy breasts and full hips. I had found myself wishing that I could switch things so that it was me that the men noticed in restaurants. It seemed ironic that Lydia's body was always in fashion—lush was "in" when she was sixteen and now thin was "in" at forty-six. My own body had developed backwards.

I am jarred back into the moment as I glimpse a man emerging from Lydia's house. As he walks slowly down the drive towards the street, I recognize Doug's broad frame. I slump down behind the wheel praying he won't see me, but the street light next to my car feels like a new sun shining on my freshly waxed white Honda.

I close my eyes and pray he'll go back in the house before Lydia gets here. Moments later a knocking on my window sends me into a panic.

"Claire, what the hell are you doing here?" Doug's face is pressed up against the car window like a ridiculous close-up in a daytime soap opera....the camera has zoomed in for a meaningful glance. "Why are you trying to hide from me?"

I sit up in the seat and open the window. It is impossible to sound casual but I give it a try.

"Hi, Doug."

"What is going on here? Where is Lydia?"

Good questions, I think, wishing I could just tell him the truth and go home. I force my eyes up to meet his. His glasses sit crooked on his nose; his thick blond hair sticks up at odd angles. I calm myself staring into his face, distorted with anger and confusion. Taken alone each of his features could not be called handsome. His nose is too large for a narrow face. His gray eyes are small and set too close together. But the whole face gives me the feeling of looking at a friendly dog, eager for affection but alert for a sudden assault.

"Lydia and I had a terrible fight. She stormed out of my house in a rage. It was my fault really. I came over to apologize." The words come out of my mouth without much input from my brain. I find myself feeling detached, vaguely wondering what my mouth will say next.

"You couldn't wait until tomorrow? What was the fight about?"

"It's a long story," I say, absurdly thinking a simple cliché might close the conversation.

Doug opens the car door. "Come on in the house. Don't sit out here in your car." It isn't an invitation but an order.

I follow him obediently, trying to invent something that Lydia and I had been fighting about. It shouldn't be hard; we fought all the time like sisters. She would yell at me whenever I said something negative about one of her schemes, telling me what a dull life I led. I would criticize her for having so little sense of responsibility and always we would end up fighting about men—her men. None of this would make for a fight topic I could share with Doug.

Just as we reach the front door, Lydia's Mercedes comes screaming up the drive. She pops out of the driver's seat like it is the middle of a beautiful Sunday afternoon, her long dark hair freshly brushed, her make-up newly applied. She smiles warmly at Doug as he approaches her, then she spots me.

"Claire. What are you doing here?" she asks.

I'd had enough questions for one night. Once Doug's back is turned to me, I begin wildly waving my arms and making distress faces at Lydia. For a second I think she is going to burst out laughing at my antics but then the light turns on in her brain as she realizes she is in trouble. Before Doug can say anything, I run over and hug Lydia, crying about how sorry I am.

"It's my fault too," Lydia says, getting into the spirit of things.

"It all started at dinner," I say, putting my arm protectively around Lydia and turning us both to face Doug. "We were at Mario's, this great little Italian restaurant in the Marina, and I ordered fettuccini Alfredo. Lydia started telling me that all that cheese and butter was the reason I can never lose weight. I got angry with her, arguing that my body was healthier than hers because it wasn't starving all the time."

As I embellish the fictional fight, Lydia glances at me, her eyes narrowing. She is probably wondering just how much of what I'm saying is based on fact. I press my arm against her back and hold her shoulder with my hand. She is all sharp angles and edges to my touch.

Doug stands silent as I spin my tale. I can't tell if he believes me are not, but I ramble on until I have covered all the information Lydia needs to know about the events of our mythical evening together. I give her a final hug, apologize for coming over in the middle of the night and exit the latest Lydia drama.

I drive home slowly, all the tension and urgency gone. My body relaxes; another crisis has passed. But instead of feeling elated and successful as I usually do after a Lydia affair, I feel strangely betrayed. My role as the clever accomplice, the private confidant, the holder of secrets always felt romantic. It was an exciting tangent in my otherwise ordinary life. Now all I want to do is get home safely.

Mark is sitting in the living room when I walk in. "You O.K.?" is all he says.

"Yes," I reply. "Let's go to bed."

Our bodies fall naturally into one another. My back fits into his chest, his arms go around me as his head softly touches mine. I feel his weight increase against my spine as he falls asleep. Mark, a solid name, one syllable like Doug and Claire. Lydia gets three syllables out of five letters when I only get one out of six.

For twenty-six years I have shared my bed with one man. Years when Lydia traveled all over the world, sleeping with dozens of men. I slide my hand over Mark's arm. A sadness fills me as I think of Doug, lying next to Lydia, alone.

Beverly Olevin

Tea

There was little left that Elsie could call her own. In eighty-seven years she had left a trail behind her as pieces had fallen away. Born to a well-to-do family in Lithuania, her early memories were cushioned with heavily upholstered chairs and delicately carved furniture.

The abundance of her early life shattered one blurred afternoon when the police broke into their home and dragged her father away. For two days her mother wailed uncontrollably, and when the tears exhausted her, she held Elsie in her arms. "You must escape," she explained in the same determined voice she used when telling Elsie she must eat her vegetables. "They will be back soon to put me in a place called a ghetto where people live behind walls like animals." She began to rock the six year-old child as if she was still an infant. "Elsie, my baby, you can't come with me. I won't let that happen to you. It is all arranged."

Confusion and terror struck Elsie like a blow across the face. "No," she screamed, "I want to stay with you Momma. Please don't go away."

"You have to be brave for both of us now, my child. Tonight. It is all ready. Your father and I have been planning this night for months. Uncle Abe is helping us."

That night Elsie was told to be perfectly still as she lay inside a wooden coffin. Carefully packed at her feet were the only possessions that would travel with her to freedom: a Russian samovar, lace linens stitched over a lifetime, a hand-painted china tea set over one hundred years old, and all the gold and silver coins that the family had hidden in the house.

Elsie never saw her mother again. The road to freedom was long and lonely. Once across the border, Elsie and her possessions were pried out of the coffin and put on the back of a farm wagon drawn by two coughing mules. Uncle Abe gave her a last hug. "This is as far as I can go. Now you will be in the hands of our friends." The old farmer guiding the wagon tipped his worn straw hat to Elsie. His smiled revealed a mouth of blackened teeth. "This is Moishe," her uncle explained. "He is known as the Gate here in Poland because he is the entrance to the underground. Elsie, don't be afraid. There are families that stretch all the way from here to the new world. They will care for you."

Once in her teen years, safe in America, she put a map of the world over her bed and in red ink she drew a line that traced her journey across Eastern Europe, into Germany, then through Denmark to Sweden where she was put on a ship to Canada. Her mother's dream for a quick escape had taken four years. Elsie was ten when she reached Canada and thirteen when she finally would call Chicago her home.

The money was all spent, lost, or stolen before she had even reached Sweden. The Russian samovar was pawned to help pay her passage to the new world, the lace linens disappeared in the moves between orphanages in Canada. All that was left was the hand-painted tea set.

Elsie lived in Chicago for seventy-four years. She married an immigrant from Poland and they had two daughters. Each day she served her family and her friends tea in the antique cups, then carefully washed and dried each one. Not a crack or a chip revealed the many hands that had held them.

After her husband died, Elsie's oldest daughter, Rebecca, begged her to move to California with her family. "You can't stay here alone now, Mother. And anyway the children need their grandmother." Before Elsie could protest, her daughter began to carefully pack the tea set.

So at eighty-seven, Elsie found herself living in a one-room granny apartment in Los Angeles. None of the furniture was hers. It all came with the place. But she did have her tea set sitting on top of the dresser and her hot plate for afternoon tea. Her granddaughter lived only a few miles away.

The jolt hit at 6:01 a.m. 7.2 on the Richter Scale, the radio later reported. Elsie sat straight upright in bed, her eyes wide with shock. Just ten minutes later her granddaughter came breaking through the door.

"Daddy, run, run, it's the police!" Elsie screamed. "Quick, before they take you away!"

"No, Grandma, it's me, Esther, don't be afraid. You're all right."

Elsie's bed had crashed across the room into the far wall. The furniture had all toppled and drawers had spit out their contents. The small room looked as though it had been ransacked. Esther put her arms around Elsie and softly patted her back.

"Ah, here you are, tattala, the face of an angel." Elsie's breathing slowed down as she recognized her granddaughter.

"I came as fast as I could."

"An angel," her grandmother kept repeating.

"We have to go now," Esther said, helping Elsie out of bed. "There will be aftershocks and this old place isn't safe."

"Yes, we go," Elsie quickly agreed. "But wait, I am forgetting...." She looked for her tea set and found it in pieces beneath her feet. "Oh, God in heaven, help me!" She bent to gather the broken fragments but Esther stopped her.

"Grandma, please, let's go now. It's not safe." Elsie allowed her granddaughter to push her through the rubble out into the open.

They had just cleared the door when another jolt hit. Esther held her Grandmother tightly and moved her away from the house. The smell of gas was everywhere.

People rushed out of their homes. After the initial panic, they sat down in the street and waited, talking quietly. "Looks just like a refugee camp," Elsie said. Then she smiled at her granddaughter. "You saved my life."

"Oh, Grandma, you're so dramatic. You were fine. But I'm sorry about your tea set."

"The tea set, yes. It's gone. I know." Soundless tears came from her eyes.

Esther clasped her grandmother's swollen, wrinkled hands. "We'll go together and buy a beautiful tea set. We can still have tea together."

"No," Elsie said quietly, "The tea is done. It had a long life and served me well. All the people who helped me on my journey to

America, they drank from the cups. All the people I have loved in my life, they drank from the cups. It's enough."

Then suddenly Elsie began to laugh. "Don't talk about tea cups now. We don't know if tonight we will have a roof over our heads. You are a good girl, my little tattala."

"Grandma, I'm twenty-seven years old and you still call me tattala."

"When you get married, I'll buy you a tea set."

"Anything to get me married."

People stayed in the street all night. They brought blankets out of their bedrooms and talked to calm one another until dawn. Someone offered Esther and Elsie tea in coffee mugs. They held the mugs like delicate china and drank the hot healing liquid together.

**Stories previously published in literary journals
and magazines.**

• •

The Gypsy Moon • *Ms. Magazine, Sun Dog, Southeast Review* (Florida State), *America West Airlines* Magazine

Claire's Oath • *Oxford Magazine,* Miami University, (Ohio)

Neat as a Pin • *THEMA,* Metairie, (Louisiana)

Safe Light • *Portland Review,* Portland State University

The Beam Walker • *Rag Mag,* Goodhue (Minnesota)

Uncommon Bonds • *The Small Pond,* Stratford, (Connecticut)

Charlotte Corday • *MacGuffin,* Schoolcraft College (Michigan)

The Fuller Brush Man • *National Coalition,* Springfield (Illinois)

Tea • *Jewish Currents,* New York

The Black Swan • *The Noctural Lyric,* Pasadena (California)

ABOUT THE AUTHOR

Beverly Olevin's last novel was *The Good Side of Bad,* named "Best Fiction of 2010" by KIRKUS Discoveries. Her previous novel is *The Breath of Juno.* Her short fiction has been published in literary magazines across the country. Beverly is also a playwright and theater director. She was Artist-in-Residence for the UCLA Osher Lifelong Learning Institute, and received a "Distinguished Instructor Award" from UCLA in 2011. She teaches courses in acting and theatre at UCLA and University of Washington. Beverly's non–fiction publications are distributed internationally. She lives in Los Angeles with her husband Marc and her border collie Sadie.

• •

For more information please visit the author's website at
www.beverlyolevin.com

• •